DEEP OVERSTOCK

#7: Horror

December 2019

❝ No new horror can be more terrible than **❞**
the daily torture of the commonplace.

H.P. Lovecraft

HORROR - GENERAL

EDITORIAL

EDITOR-IN-CHIEF: Robert Eversmann

MANAGING EDITORS: Mickey Collins & Ariel Kusby

PROSE: Mickey Collins & Robert Eversmann & Z.B. Wagman

POETRY: Ariel Kusby

SOCIAL MEDIA: Ariel Kusby & Caroline McCulloch

WEB DESIGN: Mickey Collins

INTERIOR DESIGN: Mickey Collins

COVER: Olive Lewis

CONTACT: editors@deepoverstock.com
deepoverstock.com

On the Shelves

Letter from the Editors

Dearest readers,

We feel inclined to warn you that the art, short stories and poems collected in this issue of horror are not suitable for children, the elderly, someone who's pregnant, or anyone with a heart condition. You have been warned...

We were horror-fied at the quality of work submitted for this issue (in a good way). Within these pages you'll encounter gruesome tales that involve monsters, madness, killers, and things that are just too terrible to put into words (but someone did).

If you're still reading then turn out the lights and light a candle, grab a glass of blood-red wine, and cuddle up with your favorite form of security, whether that be blanket, pet, or significant other. It's time for some bone-chilling, spooky storytimes.

We will be announcing our next theme after the holidays.

Yours, in good times and in bad times,

Deep Overstock Editors

Harbinger
by Doug Chase

Couldn't see too well. It was my mother's living room, I knew it was, and I was sleeping on the couch, and I got up. Couldn't see hardly at all. It was a fog, but it was in my eyes.

The walls didn't have corners. Should have been a big arched opening to the dining room. Nothing, just the walls, a blue cast to them, fuzzed out where the angles should have met. That dining room, on the other side of it was the hallway that went to the stairs that went to my mother's room, but I couldn't see any of it. And my sound was fuzzed out, too, just the buzz that comes from the fridge, the fridge that should have been in the kitchen next to the dining room, the fridge that came second hand from the Vincent de Paul store downtown. That fridge now, whiter than the white of the walls around me, stood like a sentry across from the couch. Taller than me, wider than it should be, and someone took off the handle, just the lower handle to the fridge part, but the handle to the upper part, the freezer, still there, shiny silver against the ice white of the whole fridge.

I was staying with my mother the summer I moved to Oregon, sleeping on her couch. She was a professor at the U of O, Classics, Greek and Latin, all that. Got there the hard way, back to school after I was grown, didn't get her parchment until she was 60. But she had a house in Eugene, a house practically in a forest, and Oregon was everything I had hoped, everything I lost after I got out of school myself. I mean, the laundromat had overgrown plants hung up in macrame pot holders. I mean, the manager of the laundromat was Jamaican, and he had long dreads, and he drove a chocolate brown Jag. I mean, this is where all the hippies ended up, my people, and I found them at last.

But that morning, up out of the couch, something wrong with my eyes, or with the living room, or the whole house. Those blue white walls fading into each other. That fridge, the buzz from it hitting the walls, hitting me, until it was like the buzz was in me.

That feeling when something is behind you, I got it. Chill on the back of my neck, chill on my forearms, hairs rising up in static attention.

A weight on my bare shoulder.

A hand.

Fingers splayed on my skin.

I turned, but slow.

My mother. Her gray hair. Ruddy face, capillaries broken across her cheeks. Her nose, people thought she drank, it was so red, but she didn't. It was her asthma, her life of coughing and fighting for breath. It was the cigarette habit from decades before that still held her.

Her eyes were the same bluish white as the walls of the room. All the way through. No color at all, just the whites of her eyes and the cloud-covered sky of her pupils. Blind. More than blind. Helpless. The color of her eyes was the color all the way through her, the color of her thoughts. There were no thoughts. There was just the buzz, which came from the fridge, and came from the walls, and came from her.

I'm taller than my mother. Almost a foot taller. I got the tall gene. I knew her by the top of her head, the shock of white which we joked and called gray. I knew her by the angle tall people know everyone, looking down the forehead and the nose, trying to see eyes from behind the shield of their eyelids.

But that morning, in that white world with no corners, I was eye to eye with her. And she was lost somewhere. Her mind was gone. Her most precious thing, her intelligence, lost somewhere in the white.

If it was a dream, it wasn't. It was a vision.

If it was a dream, then what I'm telling you is stupid. Who wants to hear someone else's dream. And besides, I never remember my dreams. But it's 25 years later, and I haven't forgotten it.

It was a vision.

Years later, and I lived in Portland, 110 miles up the road from my mother. She still taught Latin at the University. She still lived in her house in the woods.

She called me.

"I had a cough I couldn't shake," she said.

Her lifetime of asthma, a cough she couldn't shake wasn't a surprise. Her voice was permanently husky.

"I have lung cancer," she said.

"Stage four," she said.

I became one of her support people. I lived two hours away, but I got off work to take her to tests, to chemo, sat with her while the formula made just for her burned its way into her arm, through her blood. I ran errands, went to the store, got her the kind of food she wanted, which wasn't much. Got her prunes because the chemo made her stopped up. She laughed when she told me how to find them.

"They call them dried plums," she said. "Less of a conno-tation."

The chemo didn't help. One day her heart stopped, then started again with enough time for her housekeeper to call 911. Her body kept failing, but she was as smart as ever.

She faded fast. Three months after she first told me, I got a call from a doctor at McKenzie Hospital. His professionally serious phone voice.

"You should come down, but your mother might be gone before you get here."

She wasn't gone. But it felt like she was. She was in a bed in Oncology. Machines watching her and quietly buzzing. She was hopped up on so much morphine. Her eyes were open, but they were swimming. It's the only way I can describe them. They were far away. They were in an ocean. There were no pupils that I can remember. Her eyes and her thoughts and her mind, they were lost in white with a blue cast.

She wasn't gone that day, but it wasn't long after. Her life, her vitality, her love, mostly her mind. Gone so fast.

Now I'm older. I was in my thirties when I stayed with my mother in Eugene. I was in my forties when she was taken by cancer. Now I'm sixty-one.

I had that same vision this morning. Waking up in my mother's house. Standing up from her couch. The room was white walls with a bluish tinge. A buzz from the enormous fridge against the wall. The fridge that was a sentinel. A chill through my chest. I've been here before. Déjà vu. The hair on my forearms rose up. A weight landed on my shoulder from behind. A hand. Fingers spread across my skin.

I turn slow as I can.

Eye to eye. A pleading expression.

Hair a shock of white.

The color all the way through, the color of my thoughts.

It's me.

My eyes lost, swimming, brimming, afraid.

Mindless. Helpless.

The buzz within me and without me.

Now I see.

Finished Business

by Benjamin Kessler

An unexpected inheritance—
on one condition. Just one
night, no big deal. Uncle Jim
was always such a joker. Easy
money though, flip the land after.
Someone's always building condos.

Don't be so sure, I'm told. *Don't
you know? Spooky house, that one.
Ghosts? Chock full.*

Surely not this vinyl siding
build-a-home. They must've had
it confused with the abandoned
riverboat casino, home assuredly
to many a malevolent spirit
still shooting crap.

No breath of wind moans shut
the door behind me as I stoop
to gather up the mail piled
clumsy on the burgundy runner:
Audubon Society address stickers,
Cigar Aficionado's holiday gift guide.

Toss his keys—now my keys—
into the ceramic dish with the coins,
to thine own self be true. Watch close
for moving eyes behind photos hanged
on the wall. Myself in a baseball uniform,
my kid sister blowing out birthday candles.
We were the closest he had to children.

Pick through the cupboards. Which box
of half-empty pasta triggers the secret passage?
None, of course, they only serve to hide
the half-empty bottle of brown liquor.
National Geographic's in a stack. Haunted?

Hardly, simply water damaged. Uncle Jim, dead
from diabetes, sugar shock right there
at the gouged formica table only two weeks prior.

You'll clean? my mother asks. *You'll wipe
it down if there's anything left? Anything they
missed?*

But there isn't. There are services
for that kind of thing and they were
thoroughly vetted to leave no trace,
to suck up bedsheet ghosts in a backpack
vacuum and pour them into canning jars
for cold storage.

Thumb through Van Morrison long plays,
brush cobwebs off the turntable and queue up
Moondance, running it backward with my fingers
to listen for hidden messages, but it only summons
silverfish from the baseboard who make trails
through the hardwood dust.

What else to do but tuck in for the night?
Crouch down to check beneath the fold out
Sleeper sofa—nothing but crumpled
fun-size wrappers—and nod off beneath
the afghan to *Seinfeld* reruns three to a VHS tape.
See these, with the stars on the label? These are my favorites.
There's nothing but stars.

Sisters

by Kristi Lovato

When I hear the key in the lock, I get scared. I forgot to find a place to hide so I have to jump to it. The apartment is real small but in the corner by the one window there are long curtains so I tuck myself up in them then pull them straight down so they quit moving right away.

"Can I get you a drink of water?" he asks her.

"Yes, please." She says. Her voice sounds so little. And sweet. Ha.

"Sure thing. We'll just get you warmed up and then we'll call your parents." No way he's going to call her parents but his voice sounds so kind I might believe him if I didn't know better.

"Thank you for finding me." I can still hear the sniffles in her voice. I guess she was crying when he found her. I bet he asked her if she was lost and she said yes. He was probably extra nice. Maybe he told her he was a fireman. You are supposed to trust the fireman.

Sometimes I get bored waiting. Sometimes it takes a long time and my legs get tired from standing and my breath gets tired from being quiet. But there are lots of ways it can get screwed up, so I just wait until it's time to come out. I can see her from behind the curtains.

She's going to blow it. Her hands are clenched into little fists and her voice is getting too big and mad. She wants her mom and she wants the phone but he isn't going to try to call her parents anyway, and she knows it. She doesn't even have any parents. Faker.

He hasn't done anything yet. He's just whispering and I can't hear what he's saying and this is the part I hate. His one hand is touching her hair and his other hand is grabbing on to the arm of the dirty brown chair. As soon as he does something I'll move.

There's a teeny tiny chance that he won't. That he'll realize how horrible he is and just stop. Miranda says we have to let
them.

Make that choice.

But we only have to wait until we're absolutely sure.

But I've never been not sure.

Ashley has no patience. She's already grumpy because she
has to be the worm again. She hates being the worm but she's
the littlest. His hand has slipped up her shirt now. Her eyes are
squished shut and I can tell she's making herself stand so so still
because the effort is making her shoulders shake.

I feel bad for her because I remember this part. How you
try to imagine that it's something grosser than his hand, like
bugs or worms or rats so you don't have to think about what his
hand is doing.

That means it's time.

"Stop it." I say. Stepping out from behind the curtains.
Miranda used to let me watch Wonder Woman, who I love,
because she's the only girl I'd ever seen who has powers kind
of like me. Even though she's all grown up and can stand out
in the sunshine. I try to make my voice mean business like
she does even though Miranda says it doesn't matter if they're
scared or not, in the end. Just her voice, though, not the way she
stands with her hands on her hips because one time I did and
the pervo started laughing and it took a long time to teach him
that I wasn't joking before...I made a big mess and Miranda was
Very Disappointed and we had to move. And then we had to
start all over again. It's okay, though. Every town has a list. That
was before Miranda found Ashley. Back when I had to be the
worm and the hook all by myself.

Miranda says we aren't superheroes. We're very strong, but
we'll never ever get big so people will never be out right scared
until is just about over. She says ...we are angels. We aren't here
for punishing we're here for Retribution which as far as I can
tell is just a great big word for punishing.

Anyways, it's not just about being strong. If we get to like hurting them just because we're stronger then it makes us just like them. At least that's what Miranda says. We hurt them because they have it coming. Miranda says we were made for it.

His head whips around trying to find my voice. For a moment there is confusion, then a slow smile. I know what he's thinking. I'm a bonus. That when he's done with Ashley he'll start all over with me and he won't even have to go hunting. He pulls his hand out of her shirt and her shoulders finally get still.

"What do we have here?" he says real slow like a song. He licks his lips and his forehead is wet.

"Poor Mister Taleno…" I say as I shake my head back and forth. I say it a lot lately. I like the way it sounds.

"Poor me?" his face pulls up on one side like he's calling the whole fact of me a liar. I like this part. I like the moment when they figure out they're not in charge anymore. He takes the few steps over to where I'm standing and bends down so his face is right in front of mine. "Poor you." He says, in a rough kind of a whisper that smells like an ashtray.

He says it almost sadly like he feels sorry for what he thinks is about to happen to me but his hand snatches out for a handful of my hair. "Now where am I going to put you until it's your turn…"

"It is my turn." Which does sound kind of cool. I reach out with my mind and he freezes. His mouth starts to form the question, like it always does. I must have heard the dumb "who the hell" or "what the fuck" or "oh my god what's happening" a hundred times before I realized I could just shut their yuck mouths down just as easy as their yuck hands. I snap it shut and make his hand let go of my hair. I twirl my finger in the air and he robot walks back toward the chair. I don't have to do that. With my finger. But I like how it makes them know that it's me. In charge. His eyes are big and round like he's screaming on the insides. Everything is going normal.

Except for Ashley.

Stupid, grumpy, "I'm tired of being the worm" Ashley, who launches like a big old cat from the floor, right at his shoulders. She knocks the air out of him with a giant "oof" in spite of his mouth being zipped. She hits him so hard that he flies right off of his feet and his head hits the door jamb with a sound like the biggest hard boiled egg in the world cracking open. He doesn't move and I realize that it's already done. She kicks him the side twice before her hands start to untangle. I can't believe her sometimes.

"God, *Ashley*, couldn't you just let me finish for once?" She can be such a brat. Miranda says I have to be patient because she is so young but it's not fair because nobody (not even Miranda) knows how old she really is.

I mean geez I may be only be seven and a half but I've been seven and a half for a really long time. She could be like a hundred and fifty.

"No, *Jessa*, he didn't have his grody hands all on you and you were taking *forever*." She's got some nerve. This doesn't look at all like something he did to himself unless he tripped and he is the worst ever at falling down. It's always supposed to look like they did it to themselves on purpose, because anybody could believe that some old chester got sick of living with himself and decided to flip the switch. We are in so much trouble. There's blood pooling up on the floor and I have to step back to keep my shoes from getting dirty. I swear, I'm going to kill her if we have to move again. I'm just kidding. I don't think she can get killed. Plus maybe this time I can get my own room.

"They can't all die by *wall*, Ashley." Miranda is going to be so miffed..." I let that hang there because she always tries to look so perfect and this time it is so not my fault. She lets out a roar but she's so little it sounds like a cartoon and I can't help it and I laugh out loud.

She puts her hands up like claws and runs at me and I just crack up harder because she knows she can't hurt me. I'm at least 3 inches taller and it's not like I'm some flabby old human perv. I duck aside at the last minute anyway and she hits the wall with a big old thud.

"Girls." Miranda's voice comes from the doorway and I don't think I've ever heard her sound so ice cold. "Explain to me why the two of you are fighting when there is a *mess* to clean up..."

My Idea of a Good Time

by Robert Torres

The ideal is somebody comes over. They don't have to be sexy but should at least be cute. They have delicate hands. They are holding a claw framing hammer. They wear something with polka dots. They move calmly and directly, not hurried but succinct. They climb into my bed. They massage my neck gently, let my head relax into the pillow. They brush my hair aside, pat it down until the rondure of my cranium is clearly visible. They hammer my skull until it cracks like an egg. (I'm well aware the pressure inside, the wetness of the bone, and the connections to other tissues will not make a real human skull crack like an egg, but this is my fantasy) and inside is a thick black-red pudding of brains and blood. It gets on the hammer. The pudding flings about the room as the hammer goes back up and down again. They smash my skull and its brain until the shape is gone. The assailant is clean. Their polka dots are unmarred. The hammer is filthy but they are clean and I am at peace.

The Vampire

by Bob Selcrosse

There is a young man with his grandfather. The grandfather is confined to a wheelchair. The grandson takes his grandfather to visit the vampire.
The vampire comes to the mouth of the cave. It is a rainy evening in March.

Age brings a vampire nearer to death. The blood of the old makes them less undead. They cannot die. No matter how much they drink. They just go into a coma.

They break into retirement communities. They are eight feet tall, typically, and incredibly thin.
Retirement communities ask for increased security—but the incentive is wrong.
Families deny they have grandparents at all. They keep them in a secret room and spoon feed them garlic. Every house is surrounded with garlic.
Some call it "age." Some call it "grandpa."

Typically, nurses are careless. Vampires just want to score grandpa.
They get back their reflection. Their skin takes on color.

Vampires do not live in castles but in the darkness of caves, or pitch-blackness of lava tubes.
When the age has worn off, they spill out of their coffins, malnourished and crawling, to crawl desperately towards death.
But there is no darkness darker than the black inside the coffin inside the blackness of a cave.

Vampires do not buy or sell coffins.
They dig them up from the graves with their claws.
They devour the body, what marrow is left in the bones, then drag the the empty coffin down the throat of a cave.
Because of their height, they must curl like a fetus.

The vampires have killed each other by cutting each others' heads off. When one vampire desires another vampire, she cuts off his head and makes love to it.

The young man desires to use his grandfather to gain personal riches.
He rolls his grandfather in a wheelchair. His grandfather has a glassy expression like a feeble animal.
The young man knocks on the mouth of the cave. The knock echoes as if it were a rock thrown down a well.
A vampire crawls up from the bottom.
This one is bald. He is tall and white and slimy. His skin is dimpled like the walls in a cave.
He gets down and inspects the grandfather's ankles, which are aswirl with blue veins.
He is bloodless, he says.
It was true. This grandfather was as thin as a bird.
You have cheated me, says the vampire. You will bring me the blood of your mother.
The young man's mother is very famous.
The future is desperate.
Wait—the vampire holds onto the grandfather's wheelchair. I will keep him.
The vampire descends into the cave with the grandfather.
The grandfather is rolled backwards into the cave.
The grandson watches the grandfather disappear inside darkness.

The young man stands by the cave. He shines in a light, but it hisses. He clicks it off. For only a moment, the glimmer of gold.

In a neighborhood, some rush out to kill a vampire. They find him there, beside their parked car, gazing into its mirror.
They pin him and drive a stake through his heart. The dead body of the vampire is carried away by a posse and left in the woods.
The murderers are only protecting their property.
Mortal peril, under the influence of age, is novel and unfamiliar, like the senses of touch and warmth.
Vampires drink blood then come out of the black like white lizards. They want to touch things, fear things, and stare into mirrors.

The young man does not need his mother's blood. The grandson waits, on the black hill in the night, and smokes a cigarette,

for now, the land's only light.
He waits. A small flame perks up in the distance, under a thin grey plume.
The vampires stand around a barrel fire outside the cave.
These vampires knew not to venture into the town. They stood around a barrel fire.
The young man cannot see their faces, just their movement in the light.
Maybe there are two of them, three of them.

When the fire went out, the young man went in.
Age only gave the vampires little more than an hour of conscious mortality.
After that, they became so weak, they couldn't stay upright.
They could only crawl back down into the cave and climb into their coffins.
The cave walls were moist. The way down was steep.
The young man's light was weak and only helped at making shadows.
But still he sensed the gold.

The ground leveled and he shined his light up. The cave was steep.
He shined the light on the coffins. He could do anything he could to them. He could hammer a stake in each heart. He could douse each coffin with gasoline, drip a trail back up above ground and light it.
First, he needed the treasure.
He heard someone swallow.
Grandpa, he said.
He shined the light on grandpa. The old man's neck was black with bruises. Blood leaked from holes on his ankles and under his jaw. His eyes were the color of piss.
Gold coins glimmered beneath him.
The young man looked at his grandfather. The grandfather looked back.
They had the same teeth. They had the same neck.
In the moment of death, a grandfather stares into his grandson so as never to leave the earth.

On the Way to the Riverside
by Amanda Depperschmidt

I.
In the house of the spirit,
in the hour of the mother,
we spilled the purifying salts,
sprinkled pillows with rosemary,
and from our blessings discarded to the
Vestal fire we heard
the chime of the ritual bell break through
the silence that sat in the dark.

II.
In the light of the day there is a certain green
in the moss and in the caterpillars that helps me
know numbers and feelings and reasons.
And as I run with my rabbit past empty lawns,
past rivers and old bungalows there's a feather
in place of where my heart is.
But if I remember something far, something vague,
I'll feel as though the tide somehow rolls up against me
like the hare who falls prey to her hunter.
When the night comes I'll lay awake from my hunger and
my mistakes as the hauntings that visit
shake the books from my shelves and sound out that
deafening bell as if life comes
only to those who fear it.
And when I reach out to the faces I have known through
many lifetimes who have now left me
alone in this one I won't cry out
for I am what I chose, or is it
the bells that have chosen?

Follow me down to the barren oak grove,
wrap my wrists with sisal twine,
roll my body over dead fallen leaves,
into a circle of cut branches and stone.
Seven robes closing in,

seven days lost to desert sands.
And through the hymns and the chants I begin to sense
my soul rising out of me to be replaced
with that of another.
From the north and up at the top of a tree there is
a woodpecker knocking hollowly at the trunk of
his old oak tree
while in the grove where I sat
burns a haunting light, green
as the moss and as weightless as a feather.
And if I told you would you believe that wicked bell
rang out and broke through
the circle I lay tied to.

III.
These days I find myself visited by the spirit of a girl,
wild, unsophisticated, and hungry.
She knocks at the door and spooks my dog from my porch
and I don't know if she is me or if she is another.

IV.
Swimming out to meet the sea dogs,
my white tigers rhythmic at my side,
we stir up fallen blossoms and petals,
the seaweed and barnacles bending and
rolling under our feet.
We have another two hours of daylight.
It is the last stretch of summer and
the days are long.
At the shore we snack on apples,
watermelon juice, and shrimp from the
Florida Keys.
To the north a shuttle launches.
To the east, across the ocean,
a distant relative or
a former friend,
once my mother,
twice my daughter,
wraps a bell around her cat.

V.
On the wastes digging up bones,
stars sliding backwards.
At the village out west,
the bells burn through cold white noise
as they carry my body to the riverside.

Undoing a curse
by Timothy Arliss OBrien

I knew since long ago,
    a curse walking into,
        on a saturday morning.

A reflection from a shattered mirror the night before,
    the curse crawls up,
        from the abyss,
          bald,
              210lbs,
and way too old to exist.

It knocked me out,
    with a bloody face,
        in the morning.
It burned down three thai restaurants,
    and leered over my shoulder,
        of a coffee shop,
          all afternoon.

By the spill of my red blood,
    and this red ink on paper,
      May I Be Free:

a broken mirror, a bloody face, and the bald abyss,

    staring straight through me

Slay Bells Ring... Are You Listening?

by ZB Wagman

The snow came early that year. The shortened days made so much shorter by the heavy mist that hung over the city. Merideth rarely found her way outdoors but when she did she was met by chill winds and icy walks. It was not something she sought out willingly. And yet, despite the gloom, Merideth could not keep a smile from her face.

It was only November but the holiday spirit was already beginning to show. Strings of lights twinkled out of the darkness while storefronts were sprinkled with fake snow. She could practically smell sugar cookies on the wind and late one night she swore that she heard caroling. It was beginning to look a lot like Christmas.

So Merideth was not surprised when she saw Santa ringing his bell in front of the grocery store. His red donation kettle matched the sheen of his coat perfectly. *Ho, ho, ho,* he boomed in time to his bell as he saw Merideth approach. *Spare some change for the needy?*

'Tis the season, Merideth grinned as she reached into her purse. The coins clinked merrily in the pot and Santa jingled his bell in thanks.

Merideth continued on as the automatic doors slid open, bringing with them a wave of heat. As *Jingle Bells* blasted from the store's sound system, Merideth found herself singing along. She couldn't help herself. She loved everything about the holidays.

❄ ❄ ❄

Merideth's stocking was hung by the chimney with care and holly had decked her halls for weeks. Even Blitzen, her favorite tabby, had gotten into the holiday spirit. His new ugly sweater was festooned with bells. With every move he made, a cascade of tinkles followed. Merideth laughed as the cat's face drooped in annoyance. They were sitting by the fire, wrapping gifts for family that lived on the other side of the country. A glass of wine sat within reach and Bing Crosby's face swam out from the television as *White Christmas* provided the soundtrack for the evening.

When the doorbell rang, Merideth gave it little thought. She assumed that her new upstairs neighbor had forgotten the door code. But when she swung the hall door open, she was greeted by a much more welcome sight: a group of carolers, lead by Santa Claus himself, were arranged on the stoop.

> *Hark how the bells,*
>
> *Sweet silver bells,*
>
> *All seem to say,*
>
> *Throw cares away.*

Without waiting, they launched into their first song. Each of them had a large handbell which they rang in time to the music. The song was as beautiful as it was haunting.

As it reached its end, Santa stepped forward. *Merry Christmas to you*, he called in his deep booming voice. There was a glint in his eye that Merideth couldn't quite recognize.

And to you a good night, she called back as the carolers moved on down the block.

❄ ❄ ❄

In her youth, Merideth had volunteered to be Santa's elf at the mall. She loved seeing the joy on the children's faces as they glimpsed Santa for the first time. Now, she was much too old to be mistaken for an elf but she still found an excuse to make her way to Santa's workshop. She watched as a small ginger girl clambered up into the sleigh next to Santa. Santa's current elf, a young blonde woman, went through the motions of snapping photos for the girl's over-eager parents.

As she watched the girl laugh gleefully, Merideth found herself queuing up alongside the other impatient parents. Most were too focused on their own hyperactive children to pay attention to Merideth. It wasn't until she reached the front of the line that anyone took notice.

Next, the too-skinny elf called, her voice dripping with

boredom. But when Merideth stepped forward, the glaze wiped from the girl's eyes. *We don't do cats.*

Merideth frowned. *It's okay, Blitzen won't bite.* The tabby looked down on the elf from his seat in Merideth's arms. The bells on his sweater sung as he lifted a paw to knead at her forearm.

Pets aren't allowed, the elf insisted.

Merideth wanted to slap her. But the crowd behind Merideth was growing restless. She had just wanted to share in the joy that she had seen on the children's faces. Blitzen hissed as her hands tightened around him. As she turned to go a voice boomed out across the mall.

It's okay, let her up. Santa was smiling down at her from his sleigh.

Though the elf grumbled, she let Merideth climb up and place Blitzen in Santa's lap. *Now what can I get you for Christmas?* Santa asked as the elf fiddled with her camera. Merideth was flustered by the question almost as much as by the famous questioner. Before she could even begin to conceive of a response there was a flash and the elf was scooping Blitzen away. The cat meowed as it was deposited back in her arms.

She turned, desperate to catch one more glimpse of Santa before she was forced away. As she did, she recognized the glint in his eye. *Wait, I know you!* But it was too late, the elf was pushing her out of the enclosure as Santa waved on the next child.

❄ ❄ ❄

When her doorbell rang that night, she was unsurprised to see a familiar figure dressed in red waving at her from the stoop. *You've been following me*, she said through a crack in the door.

What? Santa's eyes seemed to widen behind his big bushy beard.

You've been following me. The store, the mall, now this.

Oh…'Tis the season and all that. Santa winked at her from

behind his spectacles.

Merideth inched the door open a little more. *What can I do for you, Santa?*

Err actually, he said, his shoulders slumping. *I forgot the code.*

What?

I just moved in upstairs and forgot the door code. Do you think you could let me in? An embarrassed glow spread out behind his beard. It only made him look more jolly.

Why don't you just go down the chimney?

Santa huffed out a laugh that ended as soon as Merideth let the door slip closed. She watched his face contort behind the glass. Words came tumbling out of his mouth… words that were very un-Santa. Merideth turned her back, retreating into the festive safety of her own apartment.

❄ ❄ ❄

The golden frosting spurted out onto the cookie in a jumble. Merideth's hands were shaking with anger as she used a knife to fill in the body of the bell. She could hear the footfalls of her upstairs neighbor echoing through the ceiling. It did not sound like he was wearing his big black boots—yet another way she knew that he was not the real Santa.

Merideth brushed her hands on her apron before plugging her phone into her stereo. She turned up the volume until the imposter's footsteps could no longer be heard over the carols. She would make it right with him.

❄ ❄ ❄

She stood outside his doorway, hesitating only now at the last second. What made her think that he would accept her offering? He had been so furious at her refusal to let him inside. But she knew that she had to trust in the season. She rung the doorbell, clutching the plate of sugar cookies to her chest.

The man who opened the door looked nothing like jolly ol' Saint Nick. He was younger than Merideth had expected.

And his chin protruded from his face like an iceberg. A completely hairless iceberg.

What do you want? The question came with only a hint of belligerence.

Sorry, Merideth said. She couldn't help but notice how lean he looked. *I was looking for Santa.*

Yeah, what do ya' want?

Oh. She stared at him, still not able to connect the man before her with the rosy-cheeked figure from earlier. *Well, I made you these.* She thrust the cookies out at him.

He stared at the proffered plate for a long moment before reaching out and picking up a single cookie. It crunched beneath his teeth and Merideth stared. His mastication disturbed her. Maybe it was how much his chin waggled without its beard. Finally he swallowed.

'S good, he said reaching for the plate still in Merideth's hand.

Probably want some milk? She said with a knowing wink.

The man began to laugh. *I wish more people brought me cookies.*

I make a lot of cookies this time of year.

Oh? She could see him relaxing as he reached for a second cookie.

I could leave a plate out for you from time to time.

I would like that.

Merideth smiled. *Will do...Santa.*

He grinned and, for a second, Merideth could have sworn that she saw a twinkle in his eye.

I don't look much the part without my suit, he said as he followed his second cookie with a third.

Merideth frowned. *No. You don't.* As much as she wanted

to, there was no pretending that this was Santa. Merideth cast about for something to say. But suddenly she wanted nothing to do with this false Santa.

Well, he said. *Thanks for the cookies. I'll be sure to keep an eye out for the next batch.* But Merideth knew that there would not be another batch. This not-santa had crumbled his last cookie.

That was the moment that the tranquilizer decided to kick in. The false Santa collapsed backwards into his apartment. The thump of his body hitting the carpet was no louder than a reindeer on the rooftop.

She stepped into the apartment, shutting the door quietly behind her. Merideth noted the lack of ornaments spread throughout the place. She saw his Santa suit crumpled at the foot of the couch. A sweating bottle of beer sat on the table within reach. It was more than Merideth could handle. She closed her eyes. The faint sounds of Christmas carols could be heard drifting up through the floorboards.

Merideth opened her eyes and, with a smile, began singing.

Slay bells ring, are you listening?
In the lane snow is glistening
A beautiful sight, oh, we're happy tonight

The Naked Father

by Eric Thralby

The first time I saw my father naked, he shut the door.
When I saw him again he was sleepwalking.
Asleep, he pulled everything from our fridge and threw it on
the floor.
I stepped on an egg. He turned.
Look at me, he said.
He looked cut from stone.
Look at me, he said. I am your father.
The next man was in the shower, a shadow behind the curtain.
Dad, I said.
What's the matter, he said.
There's a man, I said.
He's a repairman, he said.
I washed my hands. The man did not part the curtain.
At night, I dreamt a naked man came in through my window
and crawled into my bed. I could not find him.
My father confronted me once before school.
Do I terrify you, he said?
I had on my boots. I had on my pants. I put on my winter
jacket.
He stood in the entryway as tall as the ceiling and naked.

Horror Haiku in Three Parts
by Dack O'llins

She is....still alive?
Color drains from her visage
Blood pools on the floor

Strapped to the chair
Innocent virgin struggles
In vain...dripping veins

Captor ... killer ... waits
Inhaling her pain ... her fear
Soon, the feast begins

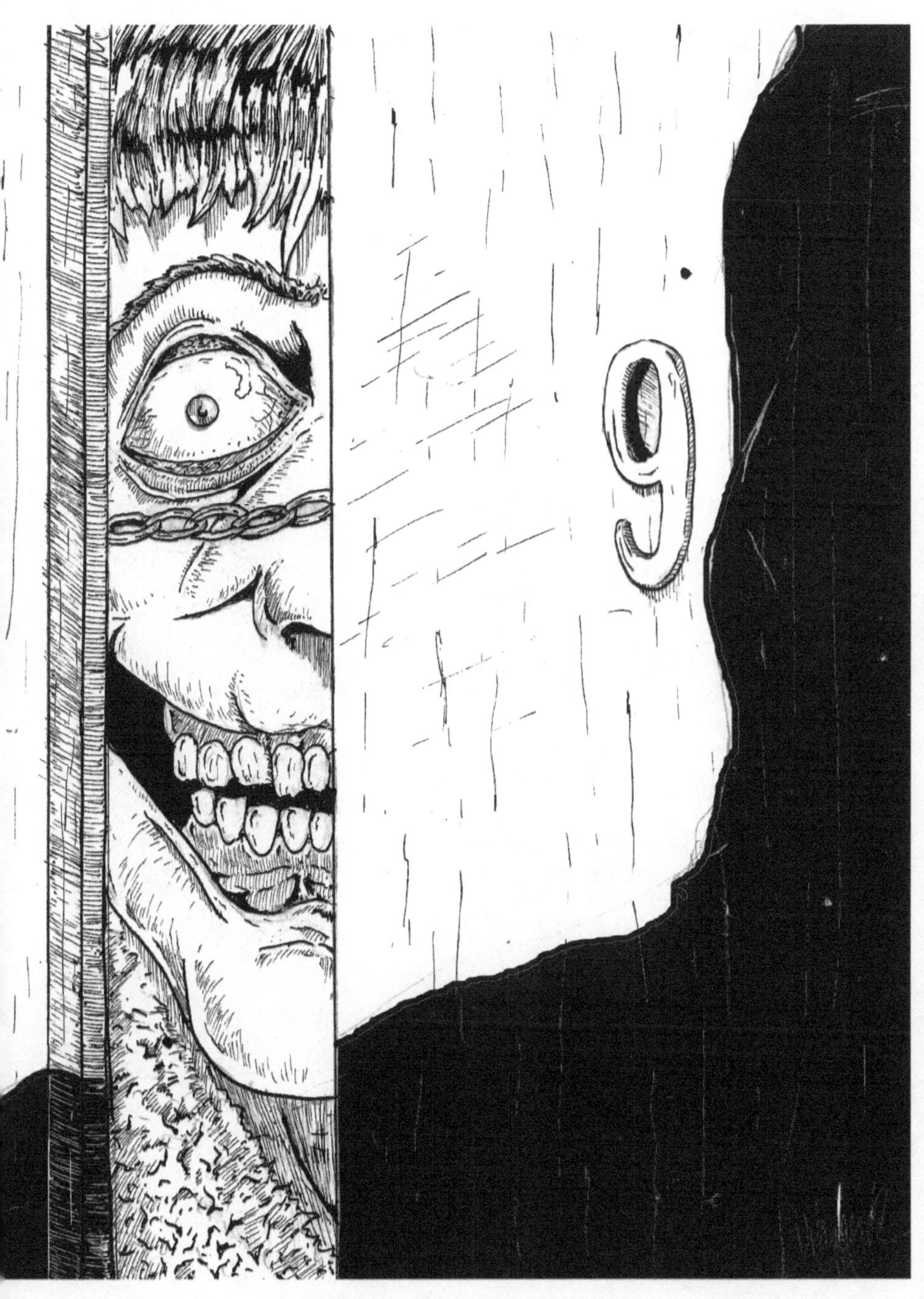

Untitled - Waylon Bacon 33

Prelude to the Afternoon of a Fawn

by Geoff Wallin

Still wet with dew
the Earth
that draws the living from the dead

now cradles newborn fawn
plays the part of grassy bed

The sun
away since yesterday
surges through the meadow

brings a thousand shades of green
drapes the fawn in hunter's shadow

Posed for death
the hunter stands and contemplates the deer

His heart cries out for life
as his arms drive down the spear

Eyes first opened days before
just glimpse the morning light

see not the horror
but watch
as newborn day turns into night

Apis

by John Chrostek

A hundred thousand moons ago,
a great blue ox as tall as the stars
would wander the sleeping expanse of Earth.
Where her hooves would fall, poppies and tall grass
would grow. Life would flourish there in blessed hues
of yellow and green, for this was the love of great Apis,
Bull of Heaven, godmother of spring.

One day in the dredges of winter, just before the season she
awoke,
two hunters found her in the splendor of repose. These men
knew nothing of the bounty of her love, her place in the cycle.
They saw meat and horns,
the instruments of power,
and set to work.

In the heavens, great Innana, Mother of All, cried a tempest of
tears,
for her precious sow had been slaughtered,
and the men now tore of her flesh.
They could not see beyond the hearth-fires
how the lush and teeming green had fallen funerary mute.

In her sadness and fury, Innana came to the hunters.
The men did not bow at the herald light
upon which she descended.
She told them at once of the sin they had committed,
placing themselves before the order,
before the spring, with this transgression,
but at this the hunter-men laughed,
their molars glimmering with red.

"The cycle begins anew, and the sow will return to the valley.
You will do as you have always done, and we shall do the same!"

Innana's anger flashed, and with a wave one hunter fell,
the flesh of his frame becoming moss and mud,
his bones both obsidian and clay.

"If you so desire to place yourselves at the beginning,
then so you shall be the end. Know this, man of might,
that though the bounty of this earth shall sate you,
it shall never save you from your fate."

And so Innana left the cursed valley where great Apis had died.
The lone remaining hunter, thinking of his people and the tale
that he would tell, took the horns of the bull on string across the
desert,
the very land the bull had meant to tread.

On his return, some knew at once where the horns
of impossible size had come from, and cursed the hunter
for his crime.

"People, you must listen!" The hunter proclaimed.
"The goddess cursed me
for not loving her in baths of star-light,
and sent this beast to slay me.
With skill and my own divinity,
I rebuked the bull of the heavens!
See how weak she proves herself to be!"

The people were for many days in doubt,
for the night sky refused all questions, the stars
sat dim on the firmament, and only the hunter's
word remained. Despite their fear of reprisal,
all the challenges of the people were memories
by the first slow coming of winter.

The great hunter soon became the lord of men
and set about remaking the world.
Pillars of stone set his kingdom high above the barren dirt,
and the people ate often and well. All
proclaimed his cunning and his might.
With care, he showed the seers of his people
where his place would be among the stars,
so as to watch over their works
in perpetuity, forever to guide them
at the beginning
of the cycle.

At the beginning, his lips would speak again and again.
But at night, in the many years before his death,
his eyes laid trace of the future, of the reach of his progeny
and the oceans of blood that they would leech.
Past that crimson sea, the yellow smoke and fire,
the eyes of his soul were left
to gaze upon the bleached white bones of the earth,
barren and dry, baring no mark or testament of life.

All cycles repeat, he prayed, in the year of his passing.
This one shall, and so shall I, until one day he watched
water funnel in a spiral, and saw the blackness of space
in the hole where the water fell out.

THERE'S SOME KIND OF BURNING INSIDE OF ME

by Mia Vicino

When I was 6, I had a tiny brown cat. Josie. As in The Pussycats. She had these cosmic eyes like inkwells, so iridescent and reflective that I swear I relived the bullshit Mirror Stage of development all over again, hypnotized into a brand new identity. Our parallel bond was solidified the night she brought a lacerated baby bunny into my room. As a gift. Cats do that. Everyone says it's because they think we're too useless to hunt, but I like to think of it as a test. Her sable eyes tacitly asked me, "How will you react to my innate need to kill?"

And I knew I was supposed to be horrified. To shriek, to run to my parents' room. But literal animal magnetism pushed me to my hands and knees, and I put my face as close as was sanitary, and I just stared. Absorbed it. The glimmering sheen of the viscera, the pallid organs juxtaposed against the cherry bomb-blood. In short, I passed.

Josie soon understood that, although I accepted her, I couldn't do the same for her gift. So she gave me a different one: the pleasure of watching her stain her whiskers scarlet, listening to her crunch bunny bones like rock candy. I tried to tamp down my rising peppery envy by forcing my brain to think the words, "disgusting monster disgusting monster disgusting monster" over and over again. But somewhere in the back of my throat, a pilot light ignited.

I'm saying this because right now, I'm straddled over the body of a bassist in a could-be-worse surf-punk band, and his blood is soaking through his flannel sheets, and for once in my life I'm not scared. Crimson is calming. I don't remember a time when it wasn't calming.

Like in my 11th grade anatomy class during dissection day. Staring at the wet mound of pale red flesh soak through the brown paper towel, I thought, "This is probably the only time you will ever touch a cow heart in your life," in blinking neon letters. "You are not good at math and science. You will never pursue this as a career. This is it."

And when my razor cut through that ropy muscle of the aortic valve, oh no, I loved it, and I hated that I loved it. When my gloved fingers probed the chordae tendinae, quite literally tugging this dead cow's heartstrings, an involuntary pang of desire slapped against my own chest. When it was over, I pulled the rubber gloves off my sweaty hands and tossed them in the overflowing trash, pausing to stare at the pile in the bin -- rubber gloves and human sweat and cow carrion that, if not for the tell-tale tang of formaldehyde, could've been blackberry jam. I imagined spreading it on toast and licking the knife clean. The coolness of the blade against the metallic flavor of the blood. Steel on iron on red on fire in me. The match was lit.

Again, just like with that mangled bunny, I knew the euphoric glow snaking between my ribs was wrong. Every primal instinct in me screamed that I should see fear and disease and death in the carnage, but somehow, on an even more ancient impulse, I saw beauty.

And that's what I'm seeing now, staring at our sanguinary reflections in this goddamn bassist's full-length mirror. I know, I KNOW slasher flicks have socialized us to associate sex with violence, but I promise you, we weren't even fucking.

A few hours ago, I'd been leaning against the back wall of some gentrified bar by the waterfront, smoking a joint and trying to look as effortlessly cool as someone trying to look effortlessly cool possibly could. There's no way I would've admitted it to myself at the time, but I was waiting for him. The bassist from the could-be-worse surf-punk band. They'd played at the bar earlier that night –– the lo-fi reverb of their effect pedals was still buzzing through my bones, generating enough buoyant energy to convince me that anything could happen. That maybe I'd better stay out late just in case the septum-pierced guy onstage slappin' his Gibson to a song called "DOOB TUBE" comes up and ask to leaves with me.

And, somehow, he did. Well, kind of. He eventually breezed out the building's back door, running his fingers through his tousled hair, and I pretended that this simple act didn't make my heart threaten to explode out of my chest, *Alien*-style. I held out my joint towards him as an offering, a way to wordlessly say, "Great show! Also, I smoke weed which is shorthand for 'I Am Cool and Chill.'" He took it without even mentioning the omen of my blood-red lipstick drenching the tip.

Then... we just talked. From the venue to his Subaru to his couch to his bed. Just talking and talking and talking. Talking until the birds sang apocalyptic hymnals outside his window. Talking until the syntax of our sentences turned to slush. Talking because the sound of each other's voices needling through the navy night was preferable to the dull, repetitive, lonely hum of the A/C.

Eventually, around the hour of the wolf, he laid his head on my shoulder, then drifted down to my chest and closed his eyes, murmuring, "You've got a fast little rabbit heart."

And I do. I do have a fast little rabbit heart. And his saying so activated it, and my hands that were lazily toying with his hair were suddenly shaking because I knew that those were the last words that would ever drip down his chin, and the implicit power embedded in that knowledge is the reason I'm picking bits of surf-punk bassist guts out of the gaps of my teeth.

There's something undeniably intimate, erotic even, about biting through a man's intestines. I thought about ending that sentence with an "isn't there?" but it's not a question. I don't need you to agree. I don't need you to approve. I've done it and you haven't. My only regret is that I called myself a disgusting monster earlier, because the pendulum is swinging back the other way. I can see clearer now, straight through to the immutable truth calcified in the marrow of my bones: There's nothing more gloriously gorgeous than a woman embracing the hunt.

WISH
by Oaktea

@OakteaParty

HMM?
HERE!
IS THAT-
IS THAT MY EYELASH...?
DID YOU JUST SWIPE THAT FROM MY CHEEK...?
YEAH!
SO YOU CAN MAKE A WISH!
WISH FOR SOMETHING GOOD.
OH GOD.
I HAVEN'T DONE THIS SINCE MIDDLE-SCHOOL.

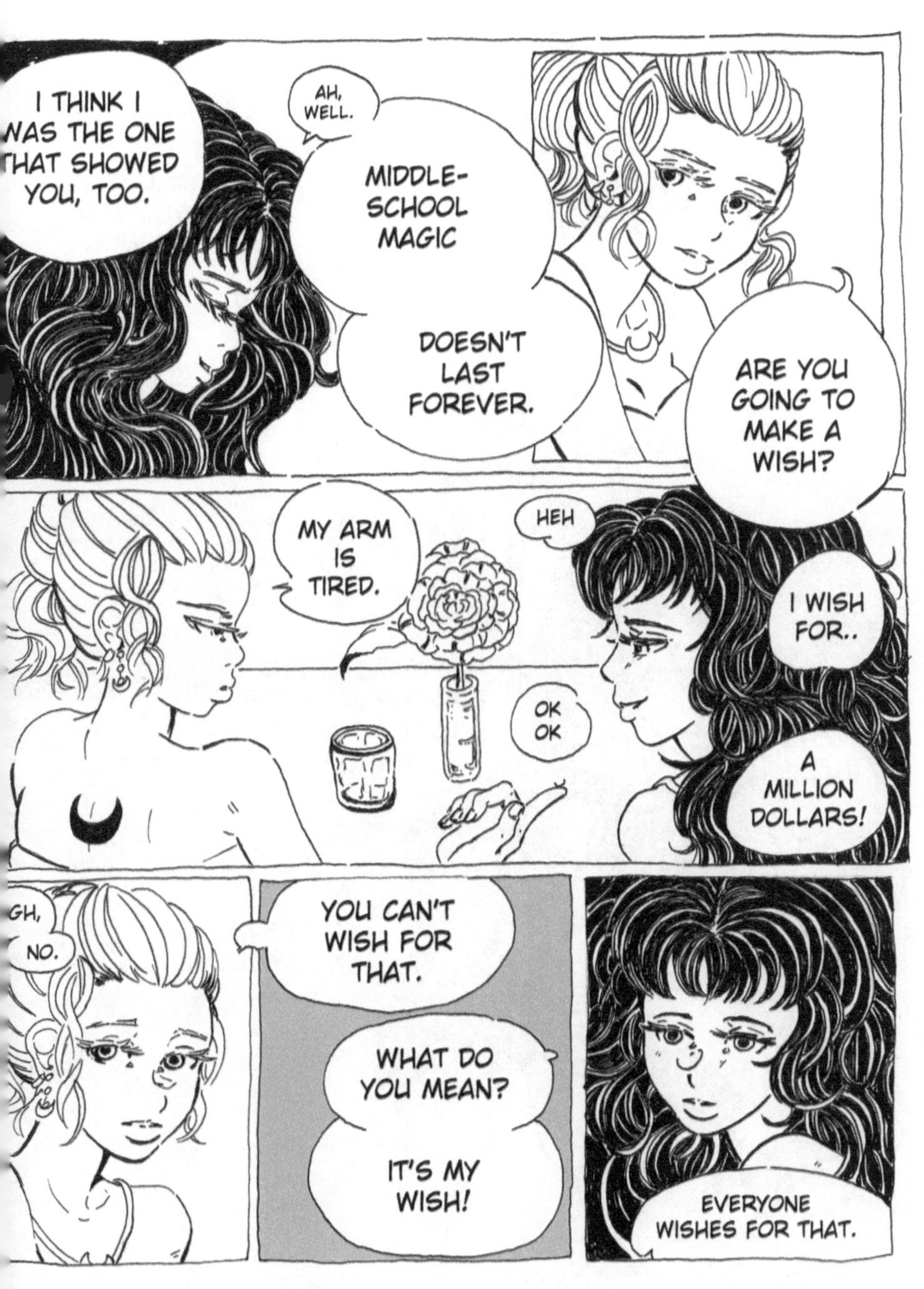

I THINK I WAS THE ONE THAT SHOWED YOU, TOO.
AH, WELL.
MIDDLE-SCHOOL MAGIC
DOESN'T LAST FOREVER.
ARE YOU GOING TO MAKE A WISH?
MY ARM IS TIRED.
HEH
OK OK
I WISH FOR..
A MILLION DOLLARS!
GH, NO.
YOU CAN'T WISH FOR THAT.
WHAT DO YOU MEAN?
IT'S MY WISH!
EVERYONE WISHES FOR THAT.

WELL,
CAN I WISH FOR TEN MORE WISHES?
...AND WHAT WILL YOU DO WITH THAT??
WISH FOR A MILLION DOLLARS TEN MORE TIMES?
LOOK.
I'M NOT THE ONE FORCING SOMEONE ELSE TO MAKE A WISH.
BESIDES,
I DON'T EVEN BELIEVE IN WISHES.
...
DO I EVEN KNOW YOU ...?

SINCE SECOND GRADE.
HOW COULD YOU NOT BELIEVE IN WISHES??
BECAUSE
FATE IS FIXED.
IT DOESN'T MATTER HOW MUCH YOU WISH FOR SOMETHING.
SOMETIMES, THINGS HAPPEN AND THERE IS NOTHING YOU CAN DO TO CHANGE IT.
YOU CAN ONLY ACCEPT WHAT IS.
WISHING DOESN'T DO YOU ANY GOOD.
BUT A WISH IS A DREAM.
AND A DREAM, YOU CAN MANIFEST, YOU CAN MAKE IT REAL, YOU CAN MOLD IT INTO BEING.
WHAT IS YOUR DREAM?
WHAT IS YOUR WISH?

I WISH...
I WISH
I WISH THAT EVERY MOMENT
THAT I HELD YOU
I COULD SAVOR EVERY ELEMENT OF YOUR EXISTENCE.
THE WAY YOU SMELL,
THE WAY YOU TASTE
THE WAY YOUR LIP QUIVERS WHEN I STROKE THE SMALL OF YOUR BACK.

I WISH THAT
EVERY MINUTE THAT I HELD YOU,
IT WOULD EXPAND INTO
A MILLION, BILLION OTHER MINUTES.
AN INFINITE NUMBER OF MINUTES,
AN INFINITE MOMENT EVER STRETCHING
AND NEVER CROSSING OVER INTO SIXTY-ONE SECONDS.
BUT MORE THAN THAT
MORE THAN HOLDING YOU INSIDE OF A FOREVER THAT DEFIED ALL LOGIC OF SPACE AND TIME
I WISH

THAT YOU
WERE
STILL ALIVE.

End

The Cook

by Bob Selcrosse

The father of abusive sons finds a way to make his sons ac-
knowledge him.
His sons drink beer and repair things.
They monkey around the backyard.
Their father brings them beers and lemonade. They crush the
cans on their heads. He makes them cookies, which they do not
use.
'You boys are something else,' he says. He fires up the barbecue.
They take red plates and line up at the barbecue. He puts meat
on their plates. He used to kiss them on the bridges of their
noses. Now they are belching gorillas.
They put their father in a headlock. He is so thin they can lift
him.
He is nothing, they tell him. They ruffle his hair.
He brings them out a cooler of beer full of ice, then corn on the
cob.
Now he is wearing giant oven mitts.
They make a joke at their father's expense.
When they have finished the corn, they open up new beers.
They heckle their father for making them full.
We couldn't possibly eat. Are you trying to kill us, old man?
They do not laugh.
The father laughs. He is dragging out more beers.
He is getting old. He is winded.
Frightened, the boys throw empties at their father's feet and tell
him to dance.
It seems he's not sure where he is.
Eventually, he brings a new box of beers.
He has since put on a long coat and a fur hat with flaps.
The boys insist they can't eat anymore. Their father is begging
them. He has made them eat potato salad, coleslaw, biscuits,
corn on the cob.
He makes them more meat. He gives them more meat.
Their father collapses. His eyes crossed from heat exhaustion.
The boys fight to unbutton his coat but their fingers are too
thick. He struggles underneath it.
Then they see his hand is missing. He uses both hands but one
is missing. Suddenly relinquishes his coat, scared that he was

ever in it.
Lift the goddamn seat when you piss, says their father. Don't
piss on the floor. Lift the seat, you animals.
His eyes go on blinking. Under his coat, he is bandaged like a
mummy.
I've fed you boys and made you big. Now I've fed you my own
flesh and blood.
They were fed up with their father. Their necks dribbled his
grease.
Love me boys, he said. He spit [eeked] blood. For God's sake,
I'm your father.

Trypophobia
by Leanna Moxley

My throat is riddled
with holes for rocks to grow in,
little white bits.
You put your
tongue in
and I wonder, do you feel it?
Can you slip between
the filled up, crumbling,
rank red cells?

My throat is cryptic,
dead things hidden in the
moist dark.
I put my
fingers in
so you won't feel it,
The ache of holes filled
up with sharp small stones.

I found a wasp nest once,
a paper maze of
crumpled gray.
And I put my
fingers in
I split it open,
the graveyard holes spilled
spider corpses and
unformed bees.

I took the first fall
pomegranate,
ripe, red, round and firm.
I stuck a knife in,
and split
the whole thing
till the many seeds
in their many holes
spilled out red and slick.

My tongue, my mouth
the roof of it, the moisture.
I put my fingers in
and it all crumbles out
and I spit it, bloody,
in the pale porcelain of
our sink.

Where do they go?
by L. Fid

Where do they go? Where should I put them?

They reach out uncontrolled at the slightest relaxation, to wreak havoc and panic. There's no escape then. Everything is exposed. Anything can happen.

And even though nothing much ever does, it's always disturbing.

Lately I've been lucky with two close-calls. All things in threes, obviously.

Still, here we are. Again and again and again. They approach. The herd. And the stragglers, the amblers, the aggressive anglers.

Why do I look up? Why don't I keep on, head down, always?

Usually, I do. I remember and I do just that. To and from the bus, over at my part-time job, in the stores and around the complex.

I've been doing it, successfully, avoiding touching anyone with my eye feelers. And pretty damn well, I'd say. This is something I'm proud of, at least that's what I'd tell that county counselor, if I was still seeing her. It's not all shame and failure.

And when I don't keep it in, down, and tucked away, it's usually because I've decided to risk it, to take a peek, to use my eyes. Even in the city. Feelers be damned.

Like if I'm back up against a brick wall with good sight lines, light foot traffic, late afternoon.

I might, then, and I have. I probably will again.

The times I forgot, though, and stumbled past a gawking soul wound unfolding in awful recognition. Those were bad. It hurts like a kidney punch even now.

This, though, this is worse.

There are no two things. The connections are already there. The feelers, nestled amongst each other, asleep. All connected at the base. Ready for activation when things are not right.

Things are not right.

The worst is worsening. The long hall and terrible approach. No hat, hats off, they said. No sunglasses either. I scream and monkey walk up the walls. I drop to all fours and shake my head violently, no, no, no.

I stand up and resume walking.

I've been walking all along. The approaching person notices no unusual happenstance, their casual loping gait unbroken, except for an occasional toe-to-carpet stumble, quickly corrected, as if the person were dividing their attentions with a device cupped in their hands.

How could they not see my anguish, perceive the panic? I keep my head down despite the urge to blur my perception and reconnoiter to the near and far corners of the hall with a lightning fast jerk of the head.

My better judgment prevails. Any movement above my shoulders is limited to a slight side-to-side motion, which I attempt to match to my short, scuffled strides. My eyes are laser focused on the floor at the end of the long corridor, down and to the side of the looming figure's head.

I should be able to get past without an entanglement, but the proximity is alarming. The slightest deviation, an unexpected variable, and there we are, looking at each other. Just moments away, possibly, from some dumbstruck interaction -- though the horror of the feeler entanglement usually precludes that denouement.

I take a few more steps before I decide I can't continue. I stop, stoop, and pretend to look at the back of my left shoe while maintaining as wide a field of vision as possible.

The loping gait changes to a controlled shuffle and the figure draws near. I squint, turn my mouth into a tight scowl, as if espying something untoward, like gum or crap, lurking on my sole. The person passes, their brown work shoes treading a careful arc around my inspection deception.

I let loose, feelers deployed. I snake them through the murky ether, brush the feathered tips towards the retreating back, taking a measure.

My hallmate turns, instantly tense, secreting a fierce pheromone cloud for camouflage and effect. I recoil to a defensive position, feelers turning against one another in a shield of concentric circles.

Theirs are already by. An anticipatory flanking movement places them right up against my head. I squint and turn.

No! I shout. Look at this crap! Gum, on my shoe! You wouldn't think, in a place like this -- Jeesh!

That's what I meant to say. What came out was some mumbled rant.

With a loudly trumpeted exertion, I stand erect, then resume walking. I'm now favoring the left heel to keep the faux sole befoulment off the carpet.

My skin prickles. The feathered feeler tips examine me up and down for quite a while. I retreat down the hallway, slow and steady.

Finally, I perceive myself alone. Still a long ways off to the end of the hall, which seems to lead to another hall, of course.

Why? Why am I here?

I'm on the verge of remembering when a door opens inward, away, and a bright light pours into the hall not five feet ahead. Someone pops out, staring straight into my face. The door closes and the bright light is gone.

There we are. Feelers and all defenses down. Our eyes locked beneath arching brows. The first reaction at not being able to disengage, a bland perplexity. That soon passes. Our jaws contort in frustration and our cheeks rise in anguish. Eyes well. The clarity is awful and piercing.

A spiral vacuum pours all matter into your head. You are consumed, desiccated into a shriveled corpse, then dust. I look back to where I was and see I am gone, part of the dust. I try to reconstitute myself and create a hideous homunculus from the scattered debris.

I'm eating dusty bone fragments when you blink and shake out the vision.

I start coughing and bend over. You ask if I am all right.

I mumble something and start walking, hunched over, staring down, away. I focus on the metal doors as I shuffle past. Most have safety glass windows, but all seem shuttered with blinds, fabric, or makeshift blocking paper and tape.

I've forgotten why I am here and what this place is. I feel winded, gut punched from the encounter and the vision. After a few steps, I manage to pull myself up and walk aright in an awkward gait. When we're perpendicular, the connection recurs with sparks and acid. We pass, painfully.

The feelers stay asleep. The worst has already occurred on the other side, so why bother, I suppose. Who can fathom?

I walk on, on. After I realize I cannot ascertain the nomenclature used to differentiate the rooms, I begin to feel disoriented, in vertigo, immersed in an infinite sameness, a platonic ideal of doors and halls, until, at last, I identify a lifeline in the descending numerals embossed atop each doorway's frame. Soon enough, though, the false end, another hallway leading far away in both directions. I turn left, towards the imaginary sole dirt. It is all the same, I think. It is. The same.

A series of jarring sounds raise hell from behind.

KaThunk. Splurt. Thrawp.

Excuse me. Do you mind if we ask you a few questions?

The medium is clouded already. My feelers dive into an amber mist, throbbing in sympathetic alarm. The contours of a suddenly shared space contract into sharp edges, amplifying the awful sense of pending violence.

Doors open fore and aft. So many feelers, angry fumes, steamers spewing light hoses, all at me. Stop. Police. I curl into a shell on the floor. I pull a plastic bus pass out of my flannel shirt and try to shoo the insistent feathers off my back.

A dollop of fire spits out behind me, four more ahead. Traveling at the speed of the medium, their trajectories shimmer through waves and currents. Feelers arise, in pursuit of the elusive wakes, trying to understand, burned by the contrails. I'm looking at a tiny part of the floor now, but the colors are the brightest I've ever seen.

Stop? You stop, that's what I say.

I have a right to be here even though I don't know why. Your missiles will miss. All things in threes.

Baby's Day Out

by John Chrostek

Baby Bink
was taken.
It is all light fun.
Donna (from Twin Peaks),
she plays the mother, she
knew Old Willy had photographed
Cotwell babies since the Great
Depression (when everyone
was hungry, when many people
died), but she dared for more.
She wanted Baby Bink upon
"the daily correspondence".
This was a creature she
had made, look how *angelic*
he is, hear the music *swell*
when his blue raindrop eyes
twinkle at pathetic thieves.

There is a feeling, most scenes,
of Schrodinger's laugh track
at the constant subverted horror.
(The way
the baby slides when shoved
by a revolving door.)

There would be a fear,
real fear, if the horrors were not all
averted. The film pervades,
behind a smile, on the recurring
joke of babies almost dying,
but Baby Bink is fine, he is
an angelic child, he crawls
beneath unswerving traffic
with a smile.

Does Baby Bink
see past this fairy story?
Can he hear the orchestra

as it holds the sour notes,
see that robot gorilla rusting
in a warehouse darkness? He gets his
Boo-Boo back, the veterans
sing in harmony far younger (brighter)
than their own lungs could reach,
the cops surround the bandits,
complete defeat. We do not have
to watch a baby buried.
How else could we laugh?

The Fall and the Creation

by Michael Santiago

"I guess… I'm just afraid, Levi," a distressed outlaw said.

"You know damn well we ain't both gonna get through the night, Cassidy. Get the hell outta here already. Would ya? I'll hold him off. The time for talk is over. Get back to your family and live out the rest of your life," a panicked, grizzled man muttered.

"I can't just leave you, Levi. Not like this," Cassidy replied.

"Now, listen here, there's a good man within you but he's at war with what he aspires to be and who he used to be," Levi responded.

"I haven't changed a damn bit. I'm still a bad man. The things I've done, well, they're just unforgivable. Maybe I deserve to be down here," Cassidy said.

"Cassidy, you've got no idea what a bad man truly is. A bad man doesn't go into the depths of hell trying to get riches for his family. Do you understand what I'm saying? I'm telling you to look at me. I'm the bad man. I had a girl that loved me dearly once, but I fucked that up. I had a daughter, but yellow fever took her. After all that, I couldn't find myself believing in a damn thing no more. Not even in myself," Levi muttered.

"I… I… can't do this," Cassidy spoke.

"Don't make me repeat myself, Cassidy. This thing is coming for us both, and it won't stop until it gets what it came for. Lord knows we ain't gonna get what WE came for, but there's still hope for you. You understand me? My path is coming to an end. Maybe it was fate that put me here. Maybe it was for you to see that you still got a life ahead of you," Levi explained.

"Levi, I'm half the man you are. Now what do I tell the town folk if I left my brother here to die from this sinister creature? And what of Butch?" Cassidy refuted.

"You tell them, you faced the destiny beset before you like

a warrior, a man. And, hell, Butch carved out his own destiny by giving in to his damn greed. Like he always did. Now go, brother," Levi replied.

The hesitation in Cassidy's eyes became transparent, and down to his core he knew that his fate offered only one path moving forward. His breath got heavier with each passing second, and as his eyes began to well up, he looked in the opposite direction to Levi. He placed his hand on Levi's shoulder and with a heartfelt farewell, he placed one foot in front of the other. Placing both hands on his sidearms, he kept both triggers firmly gripped.

"Most people spend their whole damn lives searching for some unattainable treasure. Nowadays, men don't realize that they're already richer than they could ever dream. Not even a man like Butch could figure that out until it was too late. The thing that keeps a man anchored is family. That's what Levi was to me. A brother. He was the only one who ever truly accepted me. Everything I know about being a man is all thanks to him," Cassidy spoke to himself.

"Never forget what happened here tonight, Cassidy. Pursue the life you were meant for. You keep running and you don't turn back," Levi's voice echoed down the halls of the concave grotto.

The creature's piercing screech drowned out the reverberation of Levi's voice.

In that very moment, a surge of recollections flooded his mind – reminding him of the man he's always been. A gluttonous killer who found himself in a vicious cycle of being misunderstood and abandoned due to his own reckoning. His ambition always exceeded his grasp, and he always wavered. He was a dreamer who idolized men like Levi, a hero both lucid and bold. In truth, he knew deep down inside he'd likely never achieve that ideal.

However, for the first time, he could see his life clearer than he ever had. He knew Levi became a hero through a series of catalysts. His courage to endure was the fabric that bound his legacy.

Cassidy halted his pace and fixed his gaze on the path he

just walked down. He shouted, "LEVI." But no response was offered. Fearing for his brother's life, he mustered up a modicum of courage to run back to Levi's last position.

As he began running back, he could hear howls and cackles seep from every crevice in the grotto. He recalled what the Algonquin tribe warned them about a fortnight ago before they embarked on this conquest.

"Sometimes the obvious path is riddled with pain and sacrifice. If the gold is what you seek, it will not come easy. Many men have turned in search of the fabled treasure inside the grotto," a chieftain of the Nova Scotian Algonquin tribe spoke.

"Turned into what exactly?" Butch replied.

"Something sinister. A wendigo. Beings that hide in plain sight, lonely places. They feast on the darkness of men. The greed in their hearts satiates them. Once you succumb to your own gluttonous desires, you rise as a wendigo. Bound to where you rose in search of new victims. Wendigo's are haggard, contorted creatures, and are cannibalistic in nature. The cycle just continues and continues. It is a cycle of falling and being created a new," the chieftain responded.

Butch and Levi guffawed at the chieftain's words. They couldn't believe what they were listening to such preposterous claims of so-called cannibals lurking in the night.

"You gotta be kidding me. You're telling me I should be fearful of some creature that supposedly lurks in that their grotto. You just want the gold for yourself," Butch asserted.

"Butch, calm yourself. We're going no matter what. We won't be swayed by an old wife's tale. Cassidy, what do you make of this? Cassidy… Cassidy…," Levi asked.

Levi's voice rattled louder and louder in his mind as he drew closer to Levi's whereabouts. Butch was taken by whatever that curse was, but that was his own doing by being so foolish. Cassidy concluded that he was not going to lose Levi as well. Nevertheless, his steadfast determination inspired his newfound courage to move forward. To abandon the moniker of killer and embrace that new man he aspired to be. A hero just like the man he was now attempting to save.

"Gahhhhh," Levi let out a blood curdling scream.

Hearing the scream, he picked up the pace to stumble across a scene so macabre and tragic it made Cassidy plummet to his knees. His heart ached as if a dagger had run right through him. Levi's body was torn apart and strewn all over the floor. He was disfigured beyond recognition.

"Cassidy, you were too late. He was claimed by the wickedness of his own soul," a cynical wendigo cackled.

"Butch, that sounds like you. Did you do this to Levi?" he said while raising his revolvers.

"Bahahaha. Yes, and his flesh was divine," Butch responded as he tossed Levi's heart at him.

Butch was clearly not completely transformed. He bore the fangs, shallow gaze, and skeletal structure, but he was speaking as fluidly as Cassidy could. Cassidy unloaded a flurry of rounds into Butch, which made him fall to the ground and gasp for breath. And suddenly, the newly turned Butch let out an unnerving howl that resounded throughout the grotto. A series of howls responded back within seconds. In that moment, Cassidy had realized that it wasn't just Butch who fell prey to his own greed and underwent a horrifying metamorphism into a wendigo. Wayward men had gone to the grotto for centuries. All warned of the same curse that was bound to the place.

"Brothers and sisters rejoice. Another joins our ranks," Butch spoke with his remaining breath.

"I'm all alone now. That same fear is settling back in, Levi. And I've never been more afraid in my life," Cassidy stated as he began to think back.

"Now we're never completely alone. Men like us, in time, will become ghosts. Relics of a bygone time. But you know what Cassidy? Fear is what keeps us moving forward. It pushes us to either become better versions of ourselves, or we cower to our own defeat. You'll know when it's time to let the old you fall so that a new, better Cassidy James can be created," Levi said over the dusty remains of a campfire a fortnight ago.

As Cassidy stepped away from the fire, he looked despondent and replied, "the thing is, I've come to see everything in a new light. I mean to say… that I'm worried that who I am will eventually place me in a position where I'm truly alone. I'm afraid of that more than anything. Losing my family. Being left alone."

As Cassidy came to, he knew that the words Levi spoke was the only way to move forward yet again. He picked himself up and staggered back down the same path he'd already gone through. Grasping the walls with a heavy breath, he was floundered.

On the other end of that tunnel, a drove of wendigo's began to dart towards him. Gnarly fangs were protruding from their emaciated grimaces. Skin tightened around their joints as if it was bound only by bone. Their eyes were lifeless and bloodshot. They were agents of sin. Beings that felt nothing beyond their own morbid slake. They now coveted the only meal they had left dwelling in the grotto – Cassidy.

He was now out of breath and had nowhere else to go. "Seven rounds. That's the only thing that's going to get me out of here. Ok, Cassidy, you got this. There's about half a dozen of those basterds ahead. Let's make Levi proud now," he spoke fervently. Catching his breath quickly, he picked up his pace and kept treading forward.

Raising one hand, he planted a round into the skull of a wendigo latched onto the ceiling. As it dropped, the remaining five wendigos became distracted by another corpse to devour. They were ravenous like a pack of feral dogs. Gnawing at the skin wrapped bones, the wendigo spared no time devouring their monstrous brethren.

"Hmph, that's the way. These things will consume their fallen," he whispered as he aimed his other revolver.

His sharpshooting days kicked in, and he dropped two more wendigos. It wasn't an isolated incident. The wendigos were tragic beings drawn to any corpse they could feast upon. With this revelation, he sprinted past the remaining creatures with the exit in sight.

Exerting every bit of strength, he had, he kept running. He didn't look back. The howls began to slowly dissipate and then he saw it. The exit. Along with three steeds still waiting out in the blistering cold. His gaze widened and a sharp grin formed.

"God damn! I did it," he bellowed as he mounted his horse.

In the darkest hour of his life, he overcame everything that held the old version of himself back, and he came out of that grotto reborn into the man he always aspired to be. Cognizant to his own evolution, he knew that Levi, had he still been alive, would be proud of the transformation that transpired in his wake. Trotting off on the back of his mount, he had finally found solace.

Instantly, a deviant claw shot up from a snowy mound and tore off one of the horse's legs. It collapsed, trapping Cassidy underneath. Howls could be heard all around the shrouded woods. His forlorn body laid on the wintry wooded canvas as the howls grew louder, and ever closer.

The Bush

by Robert Eversmann

These are men in blue jeans. They have a handle on the neighborhood.
They cultivate a bush. They hunch around and keep it secret.
They surround the bush like plumbers on a problem.
Children come over. They try to get a glimpse of the bush.
Boys peer at it.
They climb their fathers' backs. They push their fathers' legs.
This is man's work. It is not the work of boys.
Inside the bush, there is a baby.
The baby is sleeping.
The fathers could not save the others, who did not grow much past the size of golf balls.
This baby, however, has lived to full size. It is green. It slightly cries.
The men do not feed it. They need only let in sunlight.
Boys swell in groups and smash against their fathers.
We want in! We want in! demanded every boy.
No, argued the wall of fathers. Never.
So you require of us that we never experience the world?
One father grabbed his son and wrenched him in.
The baby breathes. Its foot, the stem, curls into the ground.
The boy hid his eyes.
This is a private matter, says his father. Do you see?
The fathers hope the boy will be let go. They could not do this to their sons. Their sons were scared. Their sons stood still behind their fathers.
The man's boy whimpered. The baby writhed.
The father pushed the boy to touch the baby.
The boy held onto his father.
The father forced his hand and spread his fingers until finally they touched.
They baby's skin was like a grape.
WHAT HAVE YOU DONE, it said.

In Your Dark Garden
by Ariel Kusby

All I wanted was a white sheet in a white room
and your milk body, too.

A bed where each time you'd make me a stranger
    and we could frenzy
              like moths tethered to light.

A temporary blindness, summertime.

What then of the black flowers
that grew inside, contortions

          allowed: bruises,
          slow-opening blood-lilies?

Because I was your little pressed flower, translucent
beneath
      the red sheet
where I'd always bloom but never
                quite enough.

68 *Untitled - Waylon Bacon*

MENSCH VERSUS MITTWOCH (MAN AGAINST WEDNESDAY) F.G. Hoch, 1930

by Mark Savage

Abraham Lincoln sagte: "Du kannsyt der Verantwortung von heute nicht entkommen, indem du es morgen meidest"

(Abraham Lincoln said: "You cannot escape the responsibility of today by avoiding tomorrow")[1]

The Landlady, *Mensch Versus Mittwoch*

There is a sequence in F.G. Hoch's *Mensch Versus Mittwoch* in which Eli, played with brilliant care by Emil Jannings, leaves a bar and walks drunkenly down a Berlin alleyway. He is set upon by an unseen assailant, who beats him to a bloody mess. The attack is shown reflected in the eye of a cat, who watches the action before turning away to toy with a dying mouse. It is such an extravagant piece of camera-work, stepping way beyond the usual stark theatricals of the Weimar Expressionists towards something quite new, that it threatens to rip the film almost completely away from its own narrative.[2] This

---

[1] *by avoiding tomorrow...* The landlady has, of course, got the quote wrong. When her tenant Eli points this out to her, she says: *You're still in bed at noon and I'm the one who is back-to-front?*

[2] *from its own narrative:* The only other contemporary example of something similarly striking might be *Alice dans le Pays des Merveilles* (Man Ray, 1929). My English teacher Mrs White had the poster of *Alice...* in her classroom. The image, with a Mad Hatter that looked more like the vampire in *Nosferatu* (F.W.Murnau, 1922), was pinned to the wall behind my chair. Once, during a group discussion about war poetry, I raised my hand to volunteer an opinion on the imagery used by Siegfried Sassoon. I was interrupted by laughter from Mrs White.

I'm sorry, Mark, but the way you're sitting, it looks like you're part of the poster and wearing a top hat. You look uncharacteristically sinister.

stylistic exuberance has its critics. Tony Deflower described the sequence as *an ostentatiously decorated Christmas Tree in August: beautiful, distracting, and completely out of place.*[3]

Several meanings can be inferred though, surely: by obscuring the brutality of the beating, director Hoch might be suggesting that the violence is too much for us; or, with the cat's disinterested stare, that the violence is banal; or that the viewer is complicit, because we *want* to see Eli beaten because we go to the cinema to see *action*; or all of the above. Hoch invites this kind of examination in the very next scene, too. A bloodied Eli limps into his room, and falls down on his bed. He reaches for a blanket to cover himself, but drops it. There is a knock at his door. It is his concerned landlady. She asks if he is ok. *Yes, of course*, he says. Fade to black. This scene takes two minutes. It is then shown again, in its entirety: Eli limps in, falls down on his bed. Drops the blanket. A knock at his door. It is his landlady. *Bist du ok? Ja, naturlich.* Fade to black. Many first-time viewers claim to miss this repetition, this record-skipping break of the verisimilitude. It is as if the brain corrects itself to believe that the scene only played once, similar to how it combines the information from two eyes into one picture.[4]

I didn't raise my hand in lessons after that.

[3] *out of place:* Tony Deflower, *"Hoch Deflowered," Film Styles* Vol 3 Issue 4, Summer 1975.

[4] *fade to black:* Psychologist Berndt Schwartzer, in a 1962 study, claimed that, *when shown the same film twice consecutively, subjects are likely to argue that they were different.* They also frequently feel that the second film was shorter. Schwartzer called this the *Wayback Feeling*, because a journey on a previously unfamiliar road seems to take less time on the return trip, due to the surroundings having already been seen and catalogued in the brain. I watched *Mensch...* twice. The first was at my Nan's on TV one Sunday afternoon. At the time I was drawing a picture of a soldier being shot (in careful detail), so I mostly only heard it. The second time was with broken headphones in the dark boxy TV room at the library. I was watching a German film in lieu of going to my German lesson. I felt that this excused me somehow. I came out of the library into the rain, fingering my left ear which had been bothered throughout my viewing by a low buzzing noise. I walked down the ramp to the underpass, and saw a bunch of kids from our school, their red shirts showing under their coats. I was surprised to see them, as I thought that the film would finish long before school was finished. I thought that they were bunking too, but the clock face above the town hall said it was nearly four-thirty.

To Tony Deflower, this repetition was even more egregious than the beating scene. He called it a *pointless trick*. But isn't it an imaginative evocation of Eli's concussed confusion? This is a film that is very much a meditation on the inevitability of the calendar. In this context, the repetition seems considered and absolutely relevant. Deflower's dismissal seems hasty. And when you consider the use of such stylistic devices as flashbacks and dream sequences (which are widely understood by viewers despite their inherent *falseness*), it is surprising that this kind of nuanced duplication hasn't been explored more often since.[5]

Later than I thought. I was on my own time. *Wayback Feeling.*

The group came closer, and I stood tall and sucked in my tummy. They were from the year above. Vicki was with them. She was L's best friend. She was considered more pretty than L, in the cannibalistic (and widely understood, despite never being explained) playground ranking system. But she had a blankness to her. She never smiled with her eyes. She whispered with the group, and then waved me over. She'd never acknowledged me before. *Didn't see you in German today*, she said.

No, I said.

Going to the arcade later, she said.

Maybe, I said.

We might sneak into the George after, she said.

Cool, I said. The older kids laughed.

Have you ever been in the George, one of them said.

Not for a while, I said. But I didn't even know where it was. They laughed. But they seemed to buy my story, and I walked on. I felt like the kid in *Hhhh* (Sara Gillespie, 1991) who convinces a peer that he can tell the time by the sun to the exact minute, all the while sneaking glances at his digital watch.

[5] *surprising:* Or is it? Maybe it is limited for storytelling purposes. Maybe we need new information each time. In Bergman's *Persona* (1966) an eight-minute scene is repeated, but this is so we can see the faces of both Liv Ullmann and Bibi Andersson in turn. There are any number of films containing *Rashomon*-style retellings of the same situation from different points of view. But the only example of the same scene repeated twice in *exactly* the same way like *Mensch...* that I can think of is in *Rappaport* (1982), when Alun Armstrong's depressed detective suffers a series of Deja-vu moments. They are Deja-vus for the viewer at least, as the character doesn't seem to ever notice.

Mensch versus Mittwoch 71

Hoch was rarely so bold again. As film scholar Joseph Pranden said when reviewing the downward spiral of the filmmaker's career, *the early prognosis of 'terminal genius' was premature, and with time the outlook receded to become something less spectacular.*[6] Those extreme spells of inspired sickness included *Gestalt Honey* (1932) and *Zwölf Jünger* (*Twelve Disciples*, 1935), but by the time of *Kiss Killer* in 1950, Hoch was in pot-boiler territory, and would never leave.

Hoch's departure to a new beginning in America in 1937 was actually an ending. Far from flourishing in Hollywood like his friend Fritz Lang, he struggled. But *Mensch...* is Hoch at the summit of his powers. His confident direction is fully backed by Weimar studio Ufa, and *Mensch...* was one of their last great pictures before the subsequent suppression of the Nazis.

In the film, Eli experiences the week as seven individuals, each with a distinct personality and agenda. These seven people visit him in the same sequence, over and over. At the beginning of the film, the meetings appear to be random and accidental: Tuesday runs into him in the marketplace, Wednesday in the café, Thursday at the entrance to his building. Each seems polite, at first. They all wear their own colours, but it seems as if Eli is the only one to see this. (When sitting at a table in a restaurant with his acquaintance Strom, Eli sees Tuesday and points him out. *See that man with the yellow flower on his lapel? No? Over there. The band on his hat matches it.* Strom says, *Him? It looks brown to me. Green even.*)[7]

---

[6] *Film As A Popular Art Form*, 1971, Scholar Books. I read this book at the library when I was once again bunking off school. Inside was a message. *Spoken to her yet? Y [ ] N[ ] Kissed her? Y [ ] N[ ] Tongues? Y [ ] N[ ] DH.*

[7] *it looks brown to me:* Hoch, like Gyorgy Ligeti, Franz Liszt, and Eddie Van Halen, experienced visual synaesthesia. *This scene is a recreation*, Hoch said, *of discussions with Fritz Lang about the colours of weekdays. Fritz insisted that Thursday was duck-egg blue. A scandalous lie* (*My Life In Cinema*, Hippo Books, 1963).

We learned about synaesthesia in science late that February. Encouraged, I'd started going to school more since the valentine landed on my desk. L was in my science lesson, and I now sat in a seat vacated by a kid with a long-term sickness (Rich with glandular fever? Tom with shin-splints? Rob with measles?) that offered a better view of her. Mr Harris tried to get a class discussion going, with his usual agitated energy: *Do any of you have any colour*

Each of the seven visitors has their own personality. Monday carries a red pen and a ledger. A name tag says *Gedanken Editor* (Thought Editor). He wears thick spectacles. He tells Eli that his short-sightedness is good for his job, because he only needs to look at his page, up close: *I need only see in two dimensions; across the ledger, and down the page to the bottom line.* Tuesday, more reticent, is always a few steps behind. Wednesday and Thursday often get themselves confused, but crucially never arrive in the wrong order. Friday is a boisterous drunk, Saturday too. Sunday, the only female, offers a haven for Eli.[8] She is calm and apologetic, and meets Eli in parks and cafés, trying to explain that the increasingly frightening mixture of

---

feelings like this? Anyone? Come on, people! (clap) *What colour is happiness?* (clap) *death?* (clap) *Monday?* He picked on L. She blushed. She was usually quiet in class. But after some prompting she went on to talk more than I'd ever heard her talk before. Her voice was scratchy and thin, and her sentences would periodically drift into uncertain noises, rather than come to a deliberate end. But her ideas were quite original, and I could have listened to her for much longer. To her, Monday was dark blue, Tuesday was yellow, Wednesday orange, Thursday brown, Friday green, Saturday black, and Sunday white. An animated discussion ensued, as members of the class volunteered their own thoughts. One kid disagreed completely with L's version. I put my hand up to say that I agreed with L that Tuesdays were yellow. (While I remember her spectrum well, I don't remember the rest of mine, perhaps because I wasn't as taken with the premise as she; perhaps because I was more taken with her than the premise. I do remember that none of my days were black or white, and that Saturday was, and remains, Ferrari red.) I glanced over. L wasn't looking, but Vicki was grinning at me. *We agree on Tuesday*, I thought. After that, I examined our behaviour more closely than usual on Tuesdays, looking for examples of extra rapport. One Tuesday in early March, L swung her bag onto her shoulder and it lightly hit my arm. *Sorry*, she said, and looked at me very briefly. *My fault*, I said. I began to imagine that our first kiss would be on a Tuesday, but then I realised that any focus on this idea removed six days from the calendar of potential.

[8] *a haven for Eli:* In *Anthologie de l'Humour Bleu*, (1942, Roman Books) Andre Breton said that Hoch and writer Lisbeth Heinz's characterisation of Sunday as female was indicative of a *petit bourgeois conservatism. One of the premises on which the Surrealist Manifesto was built postulated that the days of the week are all women* (p.78). It is hard to argue with such absurd defiance.

petty punctuality, brawn, and casual indifference that the others display isn't their fault. *They just do what they do, Eli. You have to understand. It isn't personal.* Eli tries to persuade Sunday to visit more frequently, maybe twice a week. But she runs away, telling him that he knows when he'll see her next. *This is how it must be, Eli.*[9]

Eli wants to run away with Sunday. He makes a plan. He figures that Wednesday is the most timid of the rest of the days. If he can avoid Wednesday he might disrupt the chain, and escape the clutches of routine. The spell broken, perhaps he'll then be able to spend weeks on end with Sunday with no threat of Monday arriving. But where can he go where Wednesday cannot find him? Week after week goes by, and there is Wednesday, following Tuesday, followed by Thursday, in the gardens, in the streets, in the woods. No refuge can be found. Eli changes his regular paths. He throws everything out of sync to surprise even himself. He loses his job and friends. *Is it a girl, Eli?* his boss says, after reluctantly firing him. *It's always a girl. No,* Eli says. *I just need more time.* But still, the days always catch up with him, and their aggression grows. Eli drinks and tries to sleep through an entire twenty-four hours, but wakes to find that one of his assailants has visited, destroying his room. *What day is it,* he asks the landlady when he gets up. She shakes her head at him. *Shouldn't you be at work?*

He resorts to a final plan. He barricades his room. He locks the door, shutters the windows, and waits. If Wednesday can't find him, Eli wins. He sits and reads. Noises occasionally distract him from his book (itself a distraction from the situation). He inspects the kitchen, the bathroom, the bedroom, then returns to sit. Repeat. Sickeningly slowly, Hoch allows us to begin to realise what Eli will, a beat or two behind us: someone else is there in his small apartment. It takes an age, but when Eli finally turns his back on the dark bedroom, Tuesday steps out from behind the long curtains. Tuesday quickly and quietly unlocks the apartment door for his eternal successor.[10]

---

[9] *this is how it must be, Eli:* It is possible to read this exchange as a warning of the organized

violence of the Nazis that was on the horizon, and the part the German people would play in

letting atrocities play out. Hoch denies this: *Critics give me too much credit. I wasn't smart*

enough to see them coming.

[10] *eternal successor:* This moment, in which Eli almost finds Tuesday, but turns away, has

They nod familiarly, their celestial relay handover as smooth as ever. And Wednesday enters, knife drawn.

Mensch Versus Mittwoch

Directed by F.G.Hoch. Produced by Franz Lammer. Written by Lisbeth Heinz, F.G.Hoch. Starring Eli Jannings, Maly Delschaft, Max Hiller, Werner Krauss. UFA/ Goldwyn Distributing Company. Release Date: November 1930 (Ger). 87 mins. Tagline: Tomorrow Won't Wait.

---

divided critics. James Anchon, writing in the *New York Times* after the film's screening at the Vision Festival in New York in 1968, complained (in the manner of many viewers of horror films ever since), that *for a man so careful to suddenly be so careless destroys the tension of the film completely and utterly.* He talks about Eli, but could mean Hoch too. Victor Perkins however, in his masterly *Film As Film* (Da Capo Press, 1972), countered that rather than being a poorly made sequence, it might represent a considered choice. Perkins suggests that Eli's oddly mannered turn away from the curtain, the one that prevents him from seeing the interloper, actually reflects a change of heart. As if Eli knows Tuesday is there, and cannot look for fear of confirming his suspicion; that he saw what he didn't appear to see: *Indicated to us by a lingering look at the floor, it is as if Eli has arrived at the conclusion that he cannot reject the sequence of events that is happening, and will continue to happen. Rather than asking why Hoch allows Eli to appear so careless when he almost trips over Tuesday's shoes but does not find him, we should ask why Eli would be so blind at such a moment. For surely it is easier to believe that Hoch the film-maker is making a deliberate decision here, that late in the day, Eli knows that Wednesday must come in. Is already here. Was always here* (p.234). Like a Greek Hero, Eli's fate was cast the moment he tried to fight. He is a man who sees things others cannot, and cannot see the one thing the others can: that one day will follow another, until it does not.

Thursday

by John Chrostek

I cannot remember my name. I do know that I am sick. I am a very sick man. I have been told by a doctor that I am frighteningly unwell and that things are looking dangerous. I do not remember what his name was, either. He was young. Vibrant. Healthy. I have not seen him in some time.

The nurse, who I see three times a week, instructs me not to leave my apartment unsupervised. She is the only person whose face I can remember clearly. She has a button nose and dimples. Deep bags under her eyes. I find her charming. She has a hard time finding the veins in my arms, but I like that, because it means she'll spend more time holding my arm. I feel her warmth beneath the latex gloves. I smile at her. I've never needed her to smile back.

The colors are changing outside, from blue and grey to yellow-red, through a wash of quiet blues until gold and violet are all that's left. It never stops being bright. The sounds of cars sweeping, screaming by, the people, all just sound like the ocean in a conch shell. I have a conch by my bed. I love my conch.

I leave the television on in the corner, but the faces, the faces are just as much an ocean as the outside. It's not enough to turn it off. I like the voices. They always sound so confident, even as they're pantomiming fear. They say Antarctica is dying. Some part of me is sad. I could have built a city there, been its first and only mayor. I want to be cold again. I want to lose a toe to frostbite.

The nurse tells me I am going to die on Thursday. She says it is about time, and starts to fill out paperwork beside me. I ask if she will have sex with me, as politely as I can. She says that it would be unhygienic. When she leaves, I fall asleep in the shower. It feels like rain.

The people in the morning are talking about a marmoset that bit the President's daughter. I am going through the dresser in the corner of my room. My clothes are not here. Someone has stolen my clothes. There was a jacket that I liked, a blue windbreaker. I know I liked it. I want to die in it, if I have to die. I bang on the door for hours, but no one comes.

I cannot open the windows. Have they ever been able to open? I slam my face into the glass to try and break it. The glass is thick. My eye swells up, my left one. I cannot see well outside of it. I cannot see well out of the other, but the normal way. I am only a little more blind.

Dawn. The sky is a beautiful yellow. I wish that I could make out where the clouds were, what shapes they suggest. I used to play that game with my little sister. I had a sister. Why did I forget I had a sister? I loved my sister. I took care of her. What does her face look like? What is her name? I have forgotten them. I have forgotten my sister.

I look for a phone, to call my sister. I cannot find a phone, not a single working phone. They killed the landlines, I remember now. They weren't needed any longer. I start to scream. I scream until my throat is raw. Then I take a shower.

Thursday. They say that it is Thursday on the television. My sister. I need to find my sister. I listen to the conch, the ocean. I remember being calm. Calm is good. The nurse liked calm. When I wasn't calm, she would use the shackles attached to the bed to keep me calm. I used to try and break them during the night, until I didn't need them anymore.

I hear voices outside my door. It is Thursday, after all. They must be waiting. If I lose my calm, I may die faster. How am I going to die? No one ever told me. They only ever said that death was coming on a Thursday.

A man in black enters. He asks if I believe in God. I ask him what my sister's name is. He does not know. I ask if he knows what my name is. He looks uncomfortable. I tell him it is fine. He says that God will love me when I die.

A new nurse takes his place, this one a man. He says he wants to help me die calmly. He seems sweet. Maybe it won't be so bad. Maybe my sister is dead already. Or she hates me. Why else can't I remember her? What could I have done? What could I have failed to do? I deserve to be sick. To die.

Everything moves suddenly. The nurse is scared. He looks

outside the window. Black smoke, he says. His fear seems real and loud. I get out of bed, holding my conch. I get to the window and see them.

Explosions. Orange clouds making black clouds making dust. The nurse is terrified. He says names of organizations I don't recognize. I ask him what the problem is. He says that people are dying. I say I know. I am dying. He says that it's different. These deaths aren't planned. I say the people who set the bombs must have planned it. This many bombs would *never* go off unplanned. He says the people being bombed are innocents. Does he mean that I am not innocent? What did I do to my sister? I ask him what I did. He does not pay attention. He is on his phone, a working one. He is ensuring his wife has survived.

I know then that I cannot die without remembering my sister. While the nurse is talking, I grab my conch and move towards the door. I am scared. I don't remember what the world is like outside. I have to go. So I do. I don't take time to think too hard about it. Otherwise, I might forget.

The building feels empty. I move through hallway after hallway. Some doors are open. I see inside. Those awake are at the windows, watching the bombs. There is no point for me in watching. I am dying.

I make it outside. The sky is black and brown, fire and smoke. I head towards the smoke. People are running and screaming away. They pay no mind to me. I am glad. I start to laugh. My legs feel soft beneath me. They bounce weakly off the hot pavement as I run. It hurts so badly. I laugh harder. I feel so free.

I trip and hit my face. It is hard to see through all this blood with my good eye, but I keep moving. Slower. I reach a city square. What city is this? I look at the signs for a name, but everything is ocean, blurry, red. I do not remember my city. I do not remember my home.

I see people hiding behind a storefront window, under tables. They are looking at me, motioning. A building bursts with fire on the other side of the square. I can barely see with all this sound.. A woman comes out of the store to grab me. She is screaming a name, a phrase, something. I can't hear her. There is a ringing in my ears.

I am inside the store. People are all around me. They all care so much. The woman is wiping my face, clearing the blood. Her touch is gentle and warm. She looks *so* familiar. Young. Short black hair, and moss green eyes. A smile like the cusp of the moon. Like Mirabelle.

"Mirabelle?" I call.

The woman does not react.

"Mirabelle."

The name. Her name. My sister's name.

"Mirabelle!"

I know that I am crying. I feel so weak. I know that I am lying down. Everyone is watching. I motion with my hand for the conch. I ask for it.

They say the conch is broken. I cry harder. I want to hear the ocean. I had the ocean with my Mirabelle, when we were young. We played together on the bay, where the tall ferns grew. She poked the horseshoe crabs with driftwood sticks to see if they were living. I wore a hollowed shell like an Army helmet and barked commands. It had made her laugh.

I want to hear the ocean. Let me hear the ocean. Let me *go*. It's Thursday. The doctor said I'm going to die on Thursday. Will Mirabelle still recognize my face?

The stranger holds me until I fall asleep. Today is Friday. The television says that we are going to war.

The Baby

by Robert Eversmann

Our town had become overrun with men dressed like babies. You would see them in the shadows. Even in the cold. They are not unlike the clowns of Exeter. They spread out on all fours.
They weigh from one hundred to two hundred pounds.
I met one baby in a storm in the parking light. At first I thought he was a fist. He was naked except for white underwear. There was a man in black watching from the rain in the alleyway. Presumably, this was the mother.
I ran to the baby and the man in black ran away.
Even cross-legged, the man was enormous. Rain pooled in his lap.
This is embarrassing for me, he said.
I don't live far from here.
The sky was horrible.
It's been an emotional day for me, he said.
We parked outside a castle.
The gateman opened an umbrella for me, which I understood was not to be shared with the baby.
The butler suggested I stay over.
I was provided with clothes, as was the baby.
When we emerged, we were matching.
Everyone is born from a baby, he said.
He lifted up his shirt and showed me his underside. I hadn't noticed it before. It was a baby under his arm, its face and hands under his skin, as if fossilized inside him.
I backed away.
No, he said.
He took my hand—his hands were smooth—and he pressed my fingers to the baby. I felt the beat of its heart in the pads of my fingers. It turned and moved like a snake. It pushed its hands up and spread its ten fingers to feel the tips of my five.
I am a dutiful man, a good brother, he said.
In the morning, I left with the storm. I stopped my car at the bottom of the hill.
The damage from the flooding was obvious. However, the roads now were fairly clear.
Who would take care of me now?

Stray Dog in the Valley

by Amanda Depperschmidt

The historical society kept no record of the girl's birth, just a rushed account of her finding as an infant washed up on the beach, rosy and plump as a sea urchin. Two local workers from the nuclear power plant upstream discovered her on their smoke break and promptly dropped her off during town council meeting. The council, an auxiliary meeting of the historical society, met pale-faced and ghastly, first to discuss the record-breaking heat wave and then to lay name to the new child and citizen of the valley.

"I want to name her Kathleen," said Kathleen the preservationist/zoning liaison. "And I want to name her Flappy," said Jeff the archivist/comptroller. For the first time in local history, no unanimous decision could be reached, and with no voting system in place the council ruled that the girl would have no name and would be referred to simply as the Valley Dog, and so the appropriate records were written, drawn up, and filed.

The Valley Dog lived quietly in a temperature-controlled room among the records and finding aids on the top floor of the historical society, a narrow plantation-style home at the base of the town's lighthouse. As a young girl the Valley Dog held onto melancholy as the soil holds onto water, awash with confusion and inhibition. After five sweltering years in the attic, the shoreline grew higher and the historical society added a third floor for the records and for Valley Dog. After another four years, the tide grew higher still and the historical society added a fourth floor to match it. Ten years more and the tide was so high that it covered the beach and reached the public parking lot; correspondingly, the historical society grew by three more floors. At the very top, the Valley Dog spent her days ensuring that the records stayed dry while her nights abided the romantic whims of a tunneler who would dig his way down from the mountains.

On the nights when the breeze broke through the heat and humidity, the tunneler would meet the Valley Dog at his tunnel gateway and lead her through the darkness to an opening at the southern ridge of the mountains. The first time Valley Dog saw the secluded grotto she gasped at a terrible but welcoming sight:

a steaming hot spring, brackish, warm, and bubbling. "My, we are so high up, and yet there is still water!" she exclaimed. The tunneler found the Valley Dog's observations amusing, and they came to frequent the hot spring and laugh and hold one another until the tunneler would fall into a peaceful sleep and the Valley Dog would dry herself off and place her ear to the ground. Each night she listened, listened for the churn she began to grow so accustomed to, deep and hot and volcanic somewhere far underground, rumbling all arterial and geothermal.

On a Tuesday, the town rained plastic. Little bits of gnarled, gnawed-on, mangled plastic. It fell down like a rainbow, gentle as snow. The members of the historical society climbed through the mountain trails to assess the strange weather and compose their records, leaving the Valley Dog to once again comb through the files and folders, ensuring that each and every document remained dry. When the society returned they brought warning of a ravaging forest fire which blanketed most of the hills and bluffs to the west of town. Sorrowfully, they handed Valley Dog a box which contained the tunneler, charred and blistered and in fourteen pieces. "Poor Valley Dog," they said, as the Valley Dog fell backwards and shattered an old vase. "Poor dumb, clumsy Valley Dog."

When the Valley Dog ran outside the plastic rain fell slowly and singularly while out west she could see the burgundy midday sky and a thick, ashy fog over the horizon. She ran across the road to the lighthouse and farther out into the grassy hills, brushing away plastic with her hands and putting her ear to the ground so that she could receive the comforting beat of the underground churn. Even then she could hear it, beckoning her towards the mountain, promising to reunite her with what she had lost. So the Valley Dog went back to the historical society, wrapped her lover's box in a linen tablecloth, and started towards the base of the mountain.

By the time the Valley Dog arrived at the foothills of the mountains her feet were cramped and bleeding. She frantically pushed past fronds and oak branches in search of her lover's tunnel but found only tousled mounds of dirt and fallen rocks. With no other choice she began her ascent upwards where the air grew hot and the ash stuck to her hot lungs like flypaper. In her hands the tunneler weighed down her shoulders, and in a moment of inattentiveness she tripped over a root and collapsed, knocking the box from her arms and flinging the tunneler all across the mountain slope. As the Valley Dog got to collecting the tunneler's calf, a wren stopped to mock her.

"Stupid girl," scolded the wren, "don't you know you're going the wrong way? The fresh air is lower in the valley." The Valley Dog grabbed the tunneler's right hand and placed it gingerly in the box. "Or," speculated the wren, "have you come to make a bargain with the mountain?" The Valley Dog weakly managed a smile and a nod, and out of sympathy for something so pathetic the wren helped her gather the tunneler back into the box and showed her a shortcut to the ridge with the hot springs. "Be quick," warned the wren, "and accept without hesitation what the mountain chooses to grant you."

A full day had past and the sun rose again over the ridges when the Valley Dog finally made it to the spring. She set the box down against the rocks and put her ear to the ground, listening for the churn, but this time she could not hear it. She sat and pondered for a moment, then carefully removed the tunneler from the box and scattered him about in the spring waters.

"I ask of you, mountain, repair my love. Put him back together pretty please, so he may talk to me again." The Valley Dog kneeled in the waters, her eyes closed and deep in prayer. She knelt until it became too hot for her to breathe, and then she plunged her head down into the water to listen for the churn. "I just want to be home," she weepily gurgled into the broiling spring. The plates of the mountain answered with a great cracking, as if coming down from the sky, as if undoing and unraveling her, twisting her spine and sinews and wringing the girl out like a soaked towel. It felt electric, sorrowful and euphoric, like lightning snapping a tree, and in the words of the wind she believed she heard her lover's voice, calling her name, a real name, and then a final flash of sentience as the waves broke against her brain, as her skull flushed out to carry the churn like a chalice.

First her feet began to boil in the water, the skin sloughing off and her muscles expanding and bloating like clouds, solidifying like bark, plunging sharp roots down deep into the earth. Then with a despairing bow the girl's arms and hands twisted and hardened into giant, reaching pincers, lightly knocking against the tunneler's left foot, forgetting phantom hands that once held each other. Finally, the girl's face contorted and twirled, excoriating a single hole, sucking air in and out, loose tongue-like tendrils reaching down to feel around the ground for bugs and scum to slurp. The girl stood up, her sunken brain more flora than mammal, and headed back down the mountain to the town, her lover left to bubble and soak in the springs.

It took the girl three weeks to make it back down the mountain, alternating between slow marching and slithering, and by the time she reached the valley the fires quelled and the majority of the plastic had been swept away. When the historical society caught sight of her grotesque form shambling down the mountainside, they quickly gathered to photograph and document her arrival, following her out and down the parking lot until she finally returned to the sea, swimming farther and farther out, awaiting a great flood or a great boil, neither the first nor the last in the purge by the uncanny earth.

Poems That Kept Me Up At Night

by Nicholas Yandell

1.

Fear is space.

Space is fear,
Compartmentalized,
Closed spaced,
Concealed.

Common spaces,
In a cold place,
Where the rest of the world traipses.

Enclosed in warmth and vitality,
A lonely,
Quarantined,
Crevice,
Where whispered echoes,
Reinforce,
Every vile confession.

Force your way through,
The hanging splinters of imagery,
And fractals of light,
Twisting words,
With salty drips of condensation,
And the sweet sickness in the air,
Alerting the nerves,
To the coming collisions,
Of steel jaws,
Inside your throat,
Ready to digest every scream.

The shadows
To be known,
Shown a state of acknowledgement.

Recognition,
As a part of you,
One that spins on the axis of emotion,
To inevitably slow down,
Straighten out,
And continue on the road to the present.

2.

Find the creature.

If I could feed it a fish,
Or a bowl of milk,
Offering all I have…

But it sputters and shakes its head.

Only when I face it,
Give it a slow blink of acknowledgement,
Can I slowly bring it the light.

Go to the door,
Carry the gleam of exposure,
Long past where the sun has reach.

Find the flexing chamber,
Through dark and winding passages,
Twitches and ticks,
And a deep hollow growl.

Below the surface,
There's no differentiation,
Between the blur of consciousness,
And night terrors.

A creature,
Torn,
From a childlike imagination.

3.

Droning low,
Like a jammed organ pedal,
Adjusted to,
Forgotten,
Only revealed,
Through shots of manufactured silence.

The muffled hum,
Of an idling engine,
Deserted,
Running minimally,
Sustaining.

Breathe,
An accustomed blend of air,
That chokes the self of memory.

Take hold of a lung,
With a thumb and forefinger,
Squeeze it to the tempo,
The thump, thump, thump,
Of a heartbeat,
Uncannily askew.

Quietly,
Unnervingly…

Dissonance,
In the acoustics,
Of this hall of suppression

Devils Postpile

by Thomas Piekarski

Eliot said that April is the cruelest month,
time of year when when lilacs were bred
out of the dead land. It's not hard to grasp
how this bleak proposition is substantiated
within the context of Eliot's unique times.
In our time we have zombie apocalypses,
children going door to door on Halloween
dressed as Dracula with his bloody fangs,
Frankenstein, Darth Vader, ugly witches.
Here in California Octobers are cruelest.
By then the state's hills have turned crisp,
which winds will whip, down power lines
and start voracious fires. Come Halloween
thousands of acres to burn north and south,
houses eradicated and people left charred.

At Mammoth Lakes Indian summer prevails
this mid October. Jewel of the Sierra range,
the idyllic Alpine ski resort a favorite spot
for haute L.A. and Bay Area elite in winter.
Monstrous Mammoth Mountain is treeless,
its ominous wide, steep, and concave slope
buried under packed snow provides thrills
for the Olympians who come to train here.
Tomorrow I'll stand up close to El Capitan
and Half Dome, in awe of sheerest splendor.
But here and now, as I check into my room
at Mammoth village, anticipation runs amok.
Under the foot of Mammoth Mountain builds
a gigantic lava dome, its magma pushed up
eon after eon. One cruel day it will explode.

I absorb its energy, am ready for the rapture.
I'd like to watch from aside as the caldera
blasts more powerfully than a billion bombs.
I want to see Earth's miraculous entrails sky.
No lilacs in the fields, but many wildflowers
purvey superb emoluments. Minaret spires

can be viewed from the overlook near town.
Eyes jet across miles unto peaks sheared by
glaciers end of the last ice age. Take note of
an earthquake fault made when Inyo craters
erupted. Discover little hidden lakes where
you may see people fishing, photographing,
canoeing, having a picnic, or in silent prayer.
Pretend you will never be dead, that no devil
could ever make you shed the fleece of time.

Early morning I step out onto the motel deck,
sun gradually rising above the tall Ponderosas.
Streetlights still beam. I scan pavement below,
learn that at 9000 feet in the Sierra it can get
plenty chilly even during an Indian summer.
Alas, Devils Postpile is waiting for me. So I
get in high gear, shower, pack, drop off key,
wondering if old Beelezebub himself might
pop up from behind some big volcanic rock.
There must be a reason they named the place
after the devil. I expect evil lurks, maybe a
pellucid phantasm that wants to steal souls
and use them to populate a horrid domicile,
one where the individual has lost all rights,
trapped in a dungeon of eternal damnation.

At the parking lot a large family of Chinese
gets out of a van in front of me, heads down
the half mile path toward the infamous pile.
They're prepared, bundled up in winter coats,
while my teeth are practically chattering, me
with only a windbreaker. I don't feel the heat
one would expect when approaching a devil's
favorite hangout. I think about how this place
is buried deep in snow all winter, impassible.
I want to reach my destination in amazement,
challenge the devil to a duel of wits if he will.
At such elevation the air is thin and my breath
a bit labored. A quarter of a mile more and I'll
arrive. Then it's an eighth mile, when at last I
countenance this rock beast and my jaw drops.

Sixty-foot-tall pure basalt hexagonal columns

form a quarter-mile-long wall utterly stunning.
Over eighty thousand years back lava flowed
from the guts of Mother Earth. It was so thick
with consistent mineral composition that when
it cooled it cooled slowly, and then contracted
into symmetrical pillars. Afterwards glaciers
cut the top that now resembles polished tiles.
At the base blocks are stacked, ton upon ton,
columns collapsed over the several millennia.
Had I been there when the eruption happened
I would have witnessed a genuine hell on Earth.
No sign of Satan. Who needs him now anyway?
What's done is gone. What will be not undone
by a devil's illusory and nefarious solicitation.

In *Les Misérables* the despicable villain, officer
Javert, didn't have it in him to forgive the lowly
beggar Jean Valjean for stealing a loaf of bread
to feed his famished kin. When no bread is left
to feed humanity, when the sixth extinction has
reached the point of no return, and species drop
like flies into a hellish aftermath of past thought,
then we will feel the anguish penitent Javert did
when he leapt to his death and his soul lamented
days spent down deep embracing the devil's lair.
Hugo leaves it to us to decide whether his victim
was but a product of nature, or instead prompted
by a diabolical force, supernal being boiling deep
within the bowels of Earth, hot, brisk, rumbling,
its main goal to accommodate mankind's demise.

The Problem with Lover's Lookout

by Mickey Collins

Your honor, the problem with lover's lookout isn't that I'm not ever invited. I don't even have a problem with my schoolmates going up there to makeout or whatever they do up there. The problem is that the bodies of the would-be lovers were never found.

There's a monster roaming lover's lookout.

I know this because I've seen it happen. I was at the top of the hill, waiting for my date to show. Chad and Kimberly drove up in Chad's new Chevy. I panicked and jumped into the nearby bushes. That's why you found footprints matching mine. I didn't want to ruin their date, so I hid and waited.

Anyways, I had to keep an eye on Chad and Kimberly to protect them. That's all. Even when things started getting a little PG-13, I watched so that if a monster did show up I would be ready to swoop in. But a monster didn't show up, and then things got R-rated. I'll be the first to admit that I had a natural teenage boy reaction to what I was privy to, and yet I still remained vigilant. I finished my business before they finished theirs, and I began to feel a bit of relief that a monster had not shown up. Perhaps they were safe for the night. It's one of my theories that the monster only hunts during a full moon, and that night it was waxing, but not yet full.

Chad's Chevy started up and they went back down the hill. It was getting late, and I knew my stepdad would beat me with his belt if I was any later than I already was, so I started back soon after them on my bike. When I got to the bottom of the hill, I saw that the Chevy had crashed into a tree. Chad and Kimberly weren't in the car, but the car doors were open and it looked like something had crawled out, or had been dragged out, off the side of the road. I followed the trail to a freshly dug grave. Using the nearby shovel, I uncovered the grave only to find Chad and poor sweet Kimberly entwined within. I reburied them, as was right to do. It made me think, too, that this monster must have some humanity in him, if he took the time to bury them. I took my time to hide my tracks leading to the grave, in order to give them the privacy they deserved.

You must think it awfully suspicious I didn't bike to the police station right then and there. Well, seeing as I was the only witness to this crime and, considering my involvement with the evidence, I knew I would be an immediate suspect. I would have to catch this monster alive and bring him in before I could explain the whole story.

The next day, the police found the crashed car. Faulty brakes they said. But they couldn't find Chad and Kimberly. Only I, and the monster, knew where they were. I took it upon myself to go to school and act normal. This was a brave act on its own. I had to make sure no one else thought of going up to lover's lookout again. But the rumor spread that Chad and Kimberly had eloped after their tryst upon lover's lookout, which only added to the mystique surrounding it. I knew more couples would be going there, and more couples would be killed.

After my stepdad fell asleep on the couch, I once again biked over to lover's lookout. This time I waited at the bottom of the hill, hoping to stop anyone before they got to the top. Unfortunately it was too dark for them to see me on the side of the road. I biked up the steep hill to begin my vigil over them. I would be their guardian angel.

I got to the top, tired and sweaty, and found one car still there. The windows were fogged up, it was a cold night, I could see my breath even, that's how I knew I was winded. I knocked on the window.

"What the hell?" I heard John say from inside. I heard some shuffling sounds and could see two silhouettes when the car's ceiling light clicked on. Maybe they thought I was a cop, for they rolled down the window. "What the hell do you want?" John said when they saw me. "Go away, pervert!" The other person was silent, I didn't even get a good look at them, I was so nervous.

I didn't say anything to John, which I deeply regret. I was still recovering from the bike up the hill. I went away as asked. But I felt angry. I was only trying to help and they turned me away like that. I thought about how they didn't realize how easy it would be to cut the brakes as the monster had cut Chad's. It would only take an instant of a lapse in a watch, which is what must have happened the night before.

The monster had to have gotten to their brakes before I even got there, for it was a repeat of the previous night when I biked down the hill again, and found John's car crashed into a light pole. Although this crash was farther than the Chevy, I found another fresh grave next to Chad and Kimberly's. The monster would have had to carry John and Evan a good hundred yards or so. Almost like a football player, I remember thinking. But I stopped myself. I couldn't start suspecting my fellow students. There was no way that any one at our school could have done this. This was the work of a monster, I reminded myself.

On the third night, I decided to play the role of bait. I would need a car and a date of course to complete the illusion, and for that I enlisted the help of my gorgeous classmate: she was petite, blonde, and I knew she would be irresistible to the monster. She didn't want to go along with my plan at first. I could tell she was scared just talking to me about it. She only agreed after I promised her $100 to help me out. That's how desperate I was, to get this monster.

So anyway, now that we were in a car, it was easy to get up the hill early. There were other cars around when we first parked, but I didn't risk knocking on their doors to warn them. I didn't want to scare the monster away. In order to be bait, I had to act like it. We had to go through all the motions.

I had snuck a six-pack from the fridge, and offered one to my classmate. She happily accepted. I respectfully declined any beer. I needed to keep my senses sharp. She said something about how she wanted this night to be over as soon as possible. I concurred. The sooner this monster was finished, the better. At one point I noticed that the rest of the cars were gone. It was just us now. The trap was almost set. I remembered how John's windows were fogged up. Perhaps that had something to do with the monster's attacks.

I wondered aloud how we would fog up the windows. She, on her third or fourth beer, made some lewd suggestions. I blushed. But she's the one who started it, not me. Despite what she may say her story is now. I won't go into any details, I am still a gentleman, but we were stopped mid-act by a police officer knocking on the door. The officer got the wrong idea, compounded by our differing takes on what was going on. But she was drunk.

Things just got more convoluted and confused from then on. Evidence was twisted around against me, like the pocket knife I always carry around being the "perfect" tool to use for cutting brakes, or that there was already a third grave dug and the dirt under my nails (I happen to garden at home).

The fact of the matter is, you can convict me Your Honor, but you won't stop the monster.

The Puppet
by Eric Thralby

There was an old couple who had built a boy of wood.
They taught him to walk and he fell and when they picked him up he laughed and danced.
The father, for the first time, had done something to be thrilled of. He carried his boy on his shoulders. The boy waved to the people in town.
Are you a boy?
The puppet stood on his head.
But does he live?
The puppet blew out a cake's seven candles.
As he grew, they taped him up and glued new boards in place.
Each day, he stepped boldly forward, renewed.
If he was tired, they held his hands and walked him.
If his body began to quake, they pushed him together with their hands and then polished out his bruises.
If he was damaged by rot or rain, they yanked out warped boards and nailed in clean straight ones.
They needed rope and glue and wood. They took the legs from their tables and the beams from their ceiling. The dismantled the cupboards and undid the bed. Eventually they took out the floorboards.
The boy had stopped speaking. He danced now with only half of his body, or sometimes lay lifeless.
Gradually, the old couple disassembled their roof.
Eventually, they lived in the rubble of their son.
They dug through his planks and assembled brief imitations of life which, like panhandlers, earned them a little money to eat.
They had no shelter but the body of their son and at night they felt their fingers into the various knots in the various boards, because knots in appearance resembled a soul.
They found the knobby dowel of his nose, which still had some warmth of life.
The old couple, in carpentry fingers, held the last of their son as snowflakes began softly down.

Ghost Made Flesh

by Robert Torres

Spread your arms out the way
you held her once
she grew big enough to swallow you
in one gulp. Feel first her cactus spines
across your neck and then
her gentle belly laugh.

       the joke?

          Hardwired to the dark back seat
          of a borrowed car, no one
          holds a gun to her but all
          four doors are locked. Slack-
          mouthed coyotes stare forward
                    - the light
              - the hood   - the rearview mirror
        -a stranger's hectic girlhood

There's no number
to call. You call out the last
name she sloughed off eloping
into the night, unfold it
from under the bed and skulk
with it draped over your
shoulders when you need
to wear the absence
after all day carrying it.

       I am broken,
       but not like this

Call in to your body
the small moving parts that break:
vertebra, coccyx, perineum,
proprioception, equilibrium, familiarity

       On a long dark drive in the hill
       country, encircled

by heat lightning,
the distance itself is home.
She adapts. She is spine,
shrike, and impaled meat.

Eat of her body.
Remember her soft and small.
Drink of her blood.
Remember what makes all things grow sharp in the desert.

The Undertaker

by Bob Selcrosse

I went to see the undertaker.
Get in, he said.
He brandished his shovel.
It's easy, he said.
He gave me his shovel and climbed into the hole.
Throw dirt on me, he said.
Was this a trick? Wouldn't he raise up higher and higher, the
fresh ground settling beneath him, until he was up above
ground again? This was undertaker humor. They are like the
clowns of death, pulling scarves continuously out from their
throats until we must cease to look. I put the dirt on him.
Over time, I gave him the dirt. It ceased to move.
A boy in rags, came.
Where is the grave digger? He said.
He is under one of these thousands of stones, I said.
He felt around in my pockets.
His mother appeared.
They held out little bowls. Feed us, they said. You are a daddy-
murderer, they said.
I took them back to the undertaker's household.
I washed the boy's clothing and rubbed the woman's head.
Although we are both workers in death, I, the coffin maker, am
fulfilled.
With the boy on my lap and the woman at my disposal, I ate
plenty of bread.
I made a telescope of pipe and glass. I taught my family to look
at the stars.
Then the undertaker came back from the dead.
I found him in the town, causing a riot. The many cut sacks of
flower. Hiding men under an awning.
What are you doing? I said.
I am confused and alone, he said.
I grabbed him. He was grey. His mouth opened and closed.
Why am I alive? he said.
You have come back. It's a miracle, I said.
His wife and child emerged and pelted him with stones. He
began a speech to them about love and what he'd seen under-
ground—the chiming of bells, the honking of horns, the myriad

of polka dots. He walked into the stones to approach them.
Eventually, he became a hand under a pile of stones.
I pulled him up and his hand came off. It was rubber. I pulled
the real hand underneath—also rubber.

The Prophet
by Eric Thralby

I threw my daughter into the air and she became old.
Are you a woman now? I said, bumbling her around in my arms.
She spit up water. I wiped my shirt. She clapped.
What horrible things can you tell me of the future, I wondered.
I threw her high up near the ceiling.
You've died, she said. For a few seconds she was grey and I saw fear in her eyes.
I caught her. And I put her in the stroller.
I took out the jam I kept in my pocket and fed her with a spoon.
We went to the park.
If I put her in an airplane, how far could I see?
I shivered.
I took us to a bench.
The trees, the people, the grass, and everything she knew would someday be dead.
I would be dead.
She kicked a leg out and and onto my arm.
I tickled her toes. She yawned. Did I bore her?
I threw her into the air.
Bones came out of her skin. She became a puff of ashes. Then at the top became light. A scream reemerged in her, as if in reverse. She became a little girl—I caught her.
She'd wet her pants. And I'd farted.

The Floor

by Robert Eversmann

For a time my brother lived under the floor.
We knew that if he bit us, we would die.
My father and I went finding fallen branches. We turned them
into firewood.
We kept on rubber boots. We weren't to move about the house
without them. Only once in bed could we remove them. We
never stepped on cracks.
My father filled the cracks but my brother popped them out.
I heard him running around at night. He pushed things. He
broke things. I have no idea what we kept under the house.
At night I'd see his fingers.
We're not brothers, he'd say.
Yes, we are, I'd say.
If you won't touch me, we're not brothers, he'd say.
My father played the organ to drown him out.
One day my father and I were out making firewood. He stood
in a pile where the snow had melted.
The kindling split then stopped. He banged it down. It stuck.
The axe had hit a knot. He put it down.
What's wrong? I said.
This morning there was a jay. It flew over the trees.
He showed me the body of a bird.
One night I woke up and my brother's hand was in the dark-
ness. He had removed one board altogether.
Come, he said. Mother is sick.
I would have to be broken to fit inside that hole.
Touch her, he said. Reach in. She's breathing.
He produced a second hand very different from his own.
Come here, he said.
I stayed in bed. I watched both hands.
When finally they slipped beneath the floor, I fell asleep.
When my father had finished a branch taller than our house, he
gave me the axe.
I'm going off to find one, he said. He walked into the trees.
It was then I heard my brother crying. He poked his hand
through a hole in the foundation.
Help me, he said. Help me. His arm made circles in the snow.

Bios

WAYLON BACON

Waylon Bacon works in the Fulfillment Department of Powell's Books, where he receives, pulls, and ships orders from both the store and the website. In addition, he is a cartoonist whose ongoing webcomic 'Frownland' has been featured in *Bang! Magazine* and on *Boredpanda.com*, as well as in the pages of a yearly calendar that can be purchased at our very own Powell's Books in downtown Portland, OR, as well as at Vroman's bookstore in Pasadena, CA.

You can follow his comic by visiting https://frownlandcomic.blogspot.com/, and see even more random art at www.waylonbacon.com

DOUG CHASE

Doug Chase lives and writes somewhere in the vicinity of Portland, Oregon. Doug has stories in the anthologies *City of Weird: 30 Otherworldly Portland Tales* and *The Untold Gaze*, and online at *The Gravity of the Thing*, *Nailed Magazine*, and one or two defunct sites. Doug is an Atheneum fellow at the Attic Institute and spent several dangerous years in Tom Spanbauer's ongoing fiction workshop. Doug has worked at a very large bookstore for the last 27 years and is proud to have been on the Local 5 Executive Board during its initial four years. Doug has a lovely spouse and a cat-like dog, so things are pretty good right now.

JOHN CHROSTEK

John Chrostek is a Pushcart-nominated poet, playwright and author who works at Powell's City of Books in Portland, OR. His work has been featured in publications such as *Artemis*, *River Heron Review*, and *Cathexis Press*.

MICKEY COLLINS

~~Mickey rights wrongs. Mickey wrongs rites~~. Mickey writes words, sometimes wrong words but he tries to get it write.

AMANDA DEPPERSCHMIDT

Amanda Depperschmidt is a bookseller in the PPR zone at Powell's City of Books.

ROBERT EVERSMANN

Robert Eversmann works for Deep Overstock. His website is roberteversmann.com

L. Fid
L. Fid is a member of a pseudonymous arts collective dedicated to world domination.

Benjamin Kessler
Benjamin Kessler's work has appeared, or is forthcoming in, *Hobart*, *DIAGRAM*, *Jet Fuel Review*, *Entropy*, *The Oakland Review*, *Epigraph*, *Superstition Review*, *The Masters Review*, *The Gravity of the Thing*, *What are Birds?*, and *Portland Review*. He is a former book serf at Powell's City of Books. He lives and writes in Portland, Oregon.

Ariel Kusby
Ariel Kusby is a writer and bookseller based in Portland, Oregon. She currently works in the Rose and Orange rooms at Powell's City of Books, where she pays special attention to children's books about witches, odd cookbooks, and gnome gardening guides. You can check out her writing at www.arielkusby.com.

Olive Lewis
Olive Lewis is a writer and artist living in Portland and shelving books at Powell's. They spend most of their time creating, reading, as well as dancing with fire in order to spark stagnation away and keep the light of new knowledge burning. Also, they're a big ol' fantasy nerd.

Kristi Lovato
Kristi Lovato is a Portland based writer and performer. Her work has appeared on the stages of The Mind Meld, Truth or Fiction, Tesla City Stories and The Hour That Stretches. She occasionally haunts the graveyard shift at the biggest bookstore in town.

Leanna Moxley
Leanna Moxley spends most of her time wandering in and out of fictional dimensions, often guiding others through these portals in her work as a Powell's bookseller, and sometimes as a college writing teacher.

Oaktea
Oaktea has always been in love with every aspect of a book--from the design to its contents, everything contributes to the experience. She started making comics for the all-in-one art and words combination, and eventually started working in bookstores to feed her voracious habit, as well as her love and respect for the form of the book itself.

Timothy Arliss OBrien

I am an interdisciplinary artist in music composition, writing, and visual arts. My goal is to connect people to accessible new music that showcases virtuosic abilities without losing touch of authentic emotions. I have premiered music with The Astoria Music Festival, Cascadia Composers, and Sound of Late's 48 hour Composition Competition. I also want to produce writing that connects the reader to themselves in a way that promotes wonder and self realization. I have self published several novels, and have written for Look Up Records (Seattle), Our Bible App, and Deep Overstock: The Bookseller's Journal. Check out my full discography, Where Are WE?, Piano Memories, Fear Sides and Soundbath, and my newest novel, *Dear God I'm a Faggot* at my website: www.timothyarlissobrien.com

Dack O'llins

Born on the Bayou, rolled with a Cajun Queen for awhile, chased down a hoodoo there and wishin he was a freight train. Nowadays mostly just a-chooglin' on down to New Orleans.

Michael Santiago

Michael Santiago is an aspiring author and current English teacher in Nanjing, China. He decided to get into education so that he could not only travel the world doing what he loves, but to ignite that creative spark by putting the power of storytelling into the hands of his students. His creative drive and passion for literature has helped him translate the power of books and their capacity to bestow knowledge onto his children.

Mark Savage

Mark Savage is an author and musician from Portsmouth, England. He lives in Portland, Oregon. Contact him at legendarymarkpetersavage@gmail.com.

Bob Selcrosse

Bob Selcrosse grew up with his mother, selling books, in the Pacific Northwest. He is now working on a book about a book. It is based in the Pacific Northwest. The book is *The Cabinet of Children*.

Eric Thralby

Captain by trade, Cpt. Eric Thralby works wood in his long off-days. He time-to-time pilots the Bremerton Ferry (Bremerton—Vashon; Vahon—Bremerton), while other times sells books on amazon.com, SellerID: plainpages. He'll sell any books the people love, strolling down to library and yard sales, but he loves especially books of Romantic fiction, not of risqué gargoyles, not harlequin romance, but knights, errant or of the Table. Eric

has not published before, but has read in local readings at the Gig Harbor
Candy Company and the Lavender Inne, also in Gig Harbor.

ROBERT TORRES
Robert Torres is a writer and performer based in Portland, Oregon who has
worked with Monkey with a Hat On, Gender Bomb, and Twilight Theater
Company, and has been published by *Nailed Magazine*, *1001 Journal*, *Spider
Web Salon*, and others. They worked for three years as a bookseller at Black
Hat Books in Portland. Their work explores anxiety, delusion, revolution,
and the conundrum of having a body whether you like it or not.

MIA VICINO
Mia Vicino is a film critic, screenwriter, and bookseller at Powell's City of
Books. She is based in the surreal disconnect between reality and fantasy,
where she writes for *Willamette Week*, *Much Ado About Cinema*, and film-
reviewing site *Letterboxd* (under the pseudonym "brat pitt").

ZB WAGMAN
ZB Wagman is a writer based in Portland, Oregon. When not writing, he
spends his days working at the Beaverton City Library. This might be why he
is horrified of dog-eared pages, overdue library fees, and Christmas carols in
November. (Though that last one might be an unrelated personal issue.)

GEOFF WALLIN
Geoff Wallin works at Powell's City of Books doing building maintenance.
He has worked as a reporter and now writes fiction for enjoyment.

NICHOLAS YANDELL
Nicholas Yandell is a composer, who sometimes creates with words instead
of sound. In those cases, he usually ends up with fiction and occasionally
poetry. He also paints and draws, and often all these activities become
combined, because they're really not all that different from each other, and
it's all just art right?
When not working on creative projects, Nick works as a bookseller at
Powell's Books in Portland, Oregon, where he enjoys being surrounded by
a wealth of knowledge, as well as working and interacting with creatively
stimulating people. He has a website where he displays his creations; it's
nicholasyandell.com. Check it out!